FORTITUDE
THE CANNON FODDER
SERIES BOOK 2

Andrew C. Suhrer

ISBN: 0578414294

ISBN-13: 978-0578414294

Fortitude - The Cannon Fodder Series Book 2

PROLOGUE

CALVIN Marley cracked open his eyes and immediately felt a blinding light stinging them. He let out a sigh, "Well, doesn't this feel familiar? Who the hell is there this time?"

His eyes adjusted as he saw a female doctor standing over him. She had dark brown skin, round eyes, black curly hair pulled back into a bun, gold eyes, and dark brown lips. She looked almost identical to the woman he'd seen in his hallucinations. "I was wondering when you'd wake up, narcoleptic drone. Never seen anyone get knocked out like that before," she teased.

"What is this, the future, the past? Do I know you? Wait, knocked out? Drone? I'm a fucking human being...sort of. And where's that asshole Alec Dumont? I'm going to crack his skull open! Hey, didn't you hit me with a rifle?" he snapped in confusion as he tried to sit up. The weight of an armored suit pulled down on him. It looked brand new and was covered in weapons, explosives, and extra ammo magazines. His helmet dangled from the back of his neck, and there was a rifle stuck to his torso. It seemed to be attached with magnets. The armor of the suit seemed to change color as he moved around. As he flexed his joints, the suit moved with him.

Though Calvin's body was working fine, his eyes weren't. The lights in the brightly lit room still blinded him. The doctor laughed bitterly as she answered, "You haven't traveled through time yet. That's for later. As for Alec, you'll more than likely never see him or anyone else you used to work with again. They didn't get voluntold to go on this suicide mission. You'll learn more about that later. Also, get used to being a freak of nature... well in this case freak of technology; but you get the idea. Right?"

"Just my luck. Every doctor I know is coy. So, am I in the past again, the future? Please, just tell me what's going on." Calvin twisted around to see more of the room and fell off the bed he was on. He landed on his torso with a loud thud. As his vision cleared, he looked up and saw an alien standing over him. She looked like something out of a nightmare: four eyes, a round pumpkin-like head, long limbs with two joints, skinny claw-like fingers and teeth that looked like they came from a shark. She smiled widely, "Relax. No hard feelings about Yosemite. You did me a favor, but for the record, I'm still going to get you killed. Nothing personal but got to covering my own ass."

Calvin scoffed at the alien, "Oh nice to meet you too. Wait, I thought we were trying to be independent from extraterrestrials. What the hell is up with pumpkin head ordering us around?" He propped himself up against the gray padded bulkhead. The unnamed alien looked over to the doctor, "Holly, do we really need to explain things to this dip shit? They're all going to die anyway."

"Well, fuck you too then!" Calvin shouted at her. Holly sighed rubbing the top of her head, "Please be kind to our Claw benefactor, or we'll die sooner than we'd like. The Spartans had to make a deal to keep the Vegans off our backs. They didn't take kindly to us throwing them under the bus. Us getting sent to die for them was an unfortunate part of the deal."

"You don't have to like it. You just have to put on a donkey show for me," the Claw told him while she nodded and grinned. Calvin's eyes went wide with fear as Holly told the alien, "I think you mean dog and pony show."

"We're just talking metaphors, analogies and figurativeness… right? No actual donkeys?" Calvin asked nervously as he pulled himself up further and backed toward the door. "It's not literal. Bestiality is messed up even by what little standards I have," the Claw smirked.

Calvin breathed a sigh of relief, "All right, just a

metaphor, good. So, you all are going by 'Claw' now? What happened? Stallion wasn't cool enough? Speaking of cool, we're good. Right? You said no hard feelings about Yosemite." Calvin looked at the tall alien with a guilty smile on his face. He remembered killing the operative named Yosemite earlier. She laughed while crossing her long arms, "Your actions got me a promotion! You're going to help me climb even higher up the ladder by killing everyone in front of me."

"What, can't do your own killing? And shouldn't I have briefing or…?" Calvin asked when he was cut off by the infirmary opening. In walked five others in armored suits like his own. They all wore helmets that looked like human skulls over their faces. One of them pointed at Calvin, "Is this the idiot who will be leading us?"

Holly nodded, and the woman grabbed Calvin by the arm and pulled him out of the infirmary, "Let's go, unlucky bastard."

"Idiot, unlucky?" He briefly struggled against them as he was pulled out of the infirmary and into the octagonal shaped passageway of the ship. The white lights turned off and were replaced with red ones as alarms sounded. He saw the name Leonidas repeatedly on the bulkhead as they moved along. Calvin shouted, "What happened to the Pandora and the rest of the assholes on board? Who the hell are you all supposed to be?"

"This douche bag really does ask too many questions," one of them huffed as they moved steadily along. None of them seemed in a rush as they took their time with their steps. There was an ominous feeling of dread in the air as they moved closer to their destination. Suddenly, members of the crew ran past them, scrambling to get to their stations. The intercom crackled, "General quarters. All hands report to general quarter's stations. This is not a drill...for once."

Calvin looked up with dread, "Shit. Already?"

"Shut up asshole. Also, use your heads up display to get information." One of them busted his chops as he violently flipped the helmet up and onto Calvin's head. Quickly, the names of his new team floated across his eyes. "Why in the flying hell do we all have the same last name?" he asked.

"Because this universe is cruel enough to have all of us share the same blood line apparently," the woman named Zara grumbled. The man called Hank gasped, "Wait a second. I thought you all knew what was going on!"

The man named Alan laughed, "We're all dead meat. That's what's going on. Isn't that abundantly clear already?"

"If only we could disobey the commands in our heads," Rose sighed in dread. All of them reluctantly followed the path indicated in their HUDs. The woman named Valery asked, "Besides the lack of free will, is no one worried that there's a Claw onboard? Last thing I remember is crippling their mortal enemies, killing one of their agents and getting ready to lead a rebellion against them. You remember anything differently...or at all?"

"She said no hard feelings. This is a funny way to show it," Calvin said as he started walking by himself.

Alan replied with confusion, "Wait a second. That's not what I remember. I thought things turned out differently. And why are we blindly following orders? Why can't we disobey?"

They all walked through another set of airlock doors and into a massive hanger bay. The deck was covered in nonskid and multiple lines indicating where vehicles would go. There were several exits leading to the vacuum of space. There seemed to be hundreds of giant bipedal machines in front of them standing at least 60 feet tall. They all had the form of a human with arms, legs, a rectangular torso and a round head. They had multiple boosters on the shoulders, legs and back. Each head had a single green visor, a flat rectangle where a mouth would be, and an antenna on the back of the head. His HUD told him what they were called. Hank scoffed, "Titans? We really need to stop with all the Greek references! Bad enough we're called Spartans. How original!"

"They're awesome! Why not have that name?" Valery asked him as Alan laughed, "The Greeks had perverted habits, abused slaves and were warmongers…kind of bad things if you ask me."

"You're a bad thing if you ask me," Rose scoffed at him as Valery snapped, "Let's get going already!"

They moved along the bay, making sure to stay out of the way of the large transports that moved toward black, smooth, triangular catapults that looked large enough to fit a Titan inside. Flight crews and other platoons headed to their respective stations. Everyone had on airtight suits to protect them as the air started vacuuming out. Calvin paused when he noticed someone following his every move. The man removed his helmet, showing his face.

"What the fuck? Is that…me?" Calvin asked as the stranger walked up to him. He removed his helmet, and it was like looking into a mirror. Both had skin that looked like it had been in the sun too long, short, curly brown hair in a buzz cut, gold eyes, a large jaw and strong chin. They both said at the same time, "What the fuck!"

"This shit just keeps on getting stranger. Doesn't it?" Valery pointed out. She went up and pulled Calvin away from his replicate who shouted in frustration, "So none of you know what's going on? Really? What kind of bullshit operation is this?"

"A suicide from what we've been told," Alan mockingly told him.

"I asked questions and got hurt. I think the best thing we can hope for at this point is a quick death," Zara told him as they arrived at their machines. Calvin felt small next to the large Mechs kneeling over him. Each torso opened, and a wire came down for them to grab. Zara went first and was quickly pulled upwards. She swung into the cockpit and the doors closed. The armor sealed her in. The other four did the same with their Mechs.

Calvin went up to his Titan. He looked up, marveling at the humanoid machine. It had extra weapons on the legs, arms, head and back. The skin of the machine was gray, but it seemed to adjust to the environment it would go into. All the joints looked like they could move fully and were as flexible as the humans that made them. Calvin flipped his helmet back on and grabbed the wire, allowing himself to get pulled into the machine. He hopped into the cockpit and sat down as the hatch closed on top of him. Straps came out from around the chair, securing him to the seat. He felt a jab on his neck, and his body went limp. Calvin was suddenly in direct control of the machine, using his own impulse to move it just like it was his own body. He lifted the limbs and moved them around. "Nice."

He suddenly saw a window pop up in front of him. It opened and played a video. It showed his old squad mates laughing at him, "You're on a suicide mission, fucker! Tough shit!"

"Wow… and to think, I once called them friends. Douche bags." He sighed to himself as the others pipped in the comm, "Suicide mission?"

"Totally called that one!" Alan said with glee in his voice.

Valery grumbled, "If I had to guess, we're doing a false flag operation on the Claw. Bastards will have an excuse to attack the wounded Vegan Empire. Why did anyone think it was a good idea to trust them again?"

"Greed," Zara told her.

"Is there no chance of us making it? I mean there must be a way to…" Hank gasped repeatedly in his denial. Zara shouted, "What part of suicide mission do you not understand?"

Rose mumbled, "That's crap!"

"Well at least the home system will be safe." Valery tried to look on the bright side. Alan shouted, "Those assholes just sent us off to our deaths. Screw them!"

"Let's try to live as long as possible then. Maybe we don't have to die just yet," she replied as a light flashed for them to move. They started walking through the large bay to a set of Crain transports that were pointing upwards. One by one they climbed inside of the triangular ships. Once inside, it flipped back horizontal with the flight deck. They were stacked on top of one another facing the bay doors. A countdown clock popped up in their HUDs with the numbers getting smaller and smaller. Everything was eerily quiet save a constant beeping sound. "All hands, prep for warp in five…"

"Here we go." Hank shouted. Calvin braced himself as the countdown suddenly stopped.

CHAPTER 1
FIRST WAVE
DATE UNKNOWN
GALACTIC LOCATION UNKNOWN
(CLAW WORLD)
LEONIDAS' HANGER BAY

W E'VE been waiting around to launch for five fucking hours!" Hank shouted in frustration. Calvin grumbled, "We know! You've been crying at least once every hour already. Damn!"

"Thrown out like garbage and still have to deal with hurry up and wait. Fuck my life," Rose scoffed while looking at the clock. Zara asked, "Sure none of you want to bullshit?"

"I did until you busted my balls about proper communication etiquette!" Hank shouted with his voice going high pitched in anger. Alan laughed, "What balls?"

"More than you'll ever have!" He shouted back at him. Alan teased him, "The ball sacks that slam into your face don't count as having more than me, bud."

"Happened to you, too?" Hank told him thinking it was a good slight. Alan laughed at him hard, "No. I was just messing with you. Who was the lucky guy?"

"Fuck you!" He shouted at him in frustration. Alan laughed again, "I see, private affair. That's so wonderful!"

"Shut the hell up, you annoying assholes!" Rose shouted at them, losing her temper. Alan told her impishly, "No."

"I'm ripping your tiny genitals off!" She shouted at him as she tried to get out of her cockpit. Valery stepped in, "No, you won't."

"Oh, I'm so going to do it now!" She shouted still trying to get out of her seat. Calvin thought to himself, "I'm so glad I'm not the one getting picked on."

"Oh, feeling left out?" Alan asked him. "Shit," he sighed realizing he didn't turn off his communication link.

"This is what I'm talking about when it comes to etiquette. Let it slide, and all discipline goes out the window. It's people like you that cause ships to sink!" Alan sarcastically told him. Zara laughed, "Thought it was dust bunnies and wrong color of socks."

"Still going to hurt you, fucker!" Rose told him when Valery spoke up, "We're about to launch."

"Bullshit!" She shouted at her when suddenly the

doors opened in front of them. "No shit."

All six of them were thrown up into space at once along with multiple other squadrons. Calvin felt disoriented as he guided the large transport with his impulses. The monitor showed him a 360-degree view of everything around him. Holly's voice came over the comm, "Marley, Alpha lead, all systems functioning?"

Calvin assumed she was talking to him. Rose huffed, "Still fucking lame that he's the lead!"

"Tough shit, cry baby! You're a lackey for a reason!" Holly snapped at her. "Now get acquainted with your Titans and Crains. Only chance you all have of surviving a few extra seconds."

"Seconds?" Calvin started going over all the functions of his machine while trying to maintain formation, "Okay. Energy shields for protection. Good." In addition to the shield, he also found the Titan's extra weapons: two plasma knives on the wrist, a plasma cannon built inside of the arms, two plasma cannons in the head, rocket pods on the legs and two cannons that went over the shoulders. His mechanical hands reached over and grabbed the two handheld cannons. He also noticed another two handheld weapons attached to the back as back up. Holly said impatiently, "Good. Now as much as I hate explaining things… I need to explain some things…

first, our makers suck."

"You don't say?" Valery asked her bluntly.

"I mean what kind of maker would throw their creations to the wolves like this? We're going across the galaxy to fight some aliens! For freedom, right? My ass!" Holly shouted.

Alan laughed, "You're going to bring up mommy and daddy issues now?"

Zara asked, "What the hell are we waiting on? Are we going to blow stuff up or what?"

Calvin wondered. "Holly, didn't you say something about time travel earlier?"

Holly laughed, "That's for another time. Focus on the here and now and hope Deus ex Machina works. I was just told to spit out some cryptic shit by our asshole creators."

"Deus what?" Rose asked with an attitude. Holly answered, sounding annoyed, "You know, maybe somebody or something will come save you from this hopeless situation you're in. Look, off the record; I'm trying to work on a miracle right now. Don't pester me."

"You're sounding a lot like your maker by being so vague!" Rose told her bluntly. Holly quickly snapped back with her insecurity showing through, "Don't compare me to them, you douche!"

Alan asked her sarcastically, "Why don't you do some more explaining?"

"Explain this!" She snapped at him. Hank shouted, "That doesn't even make any sense."

"You don't make sense!" She shouted at them as the comm line was turned off. Calvin grumbled, "Thanks for pissing off the only person with answers, asshole."

"She didn't have any. Also, totally worth it!" He laughed. All of them backed away from the Leonidas and got a better view of the destroyer. She was in the shape of a black Tri-Star that seemed to float through the stars with a propulsion that wasn't visible to the naked eye. The surface of the ship was smooth and rounded with pointed edges. All the ship's important systems were located at the center. The dimples in the hulls were weapons launchers. The ship could fire off in any direction at once and move in any direction she pleased.

The Leonidas was joined by several other destroyers that looked almost identical to her. There were at least forty-eight of them all together in a V-shaped formation with a quad star shaped cruiser at the head of the formation. Soon seven other formations of Spartan vessels came into view with the same number of ships. All of them had their own modified transports flying out behind them. Each vessel was painted black to blend in with the void of space. The whole fleet was heading towards a single planet.

As they got closer, the planet encompassed their whole view. The world was blue and green with white clouds drifting in the sky. It looked almost like a mirror image of Earth. Being on the dark side of the world, lights glowed from the cities on the surface. There were also several space stations in orbit. Most looked like two silver pyramids attached together by a glass covered sphere. There were fireworks going off all over. They seemed to be having a celebration.

A massive pride of Claw starships moved in single file formation right in front of them. Their hulls were highlighted in their HUDs. They numbered in the hundreds. The largest ship was in the shape of a ten-tipped star. The next largest was shaped like a six-tipped star. Their fleet ended with a single triangular shaped ship. The Spartan ships looked similar because the Claw gave them to humanity.

None of the Claw vessels seemed to react or be paying any attention to the incoming battle groups. As the fleet got closer, it increased its speed. The Spartan ships must have been using holographic imagers to conceal themselves or be using a borrowed IFF. It seemed to work as they got closer and closer to the force. Alan asked in an almost pure panic, "We're really doing this shit?"

"It's called a surprise attack for a reason. Yet, I don't think we're supposed to be surprised, too." Calvin told him as they kept their formation together. Valery quickly asked, "Is anything in this jacked up universe surprising? Be honest. Who didn't see us getting screwed over?"

"We're not dead or castrated! Take that as a good sign. Let's focus on the task at hand: avoid getting killed for as long as possible. We can regroup and worry if we're still alive afterwards," Calvin said mostly trying to reassure himself. This wasn't the first time he faced death. Might as well accept the situation and roll with it. Zara shouted, "This is fucking bullshit!"

"Well, at least we get to take others down with us," Rose pointed out as she charged up her weapons. Alan quipped, "Don't like going down alone?"

"Will you shut up?" Rose shouted at him, fear emanating from her voice. There was a sudden glow from each ship as they charged their weapons. Calvin smiled anticipating the fireworks, "Brace yourselves!"

"You're a brace!" Alan told him. Calvin smiled, "At least I'm not abrasive!"

In a bright flash of light, every ship in the attacking fleet fired at once, concentrating the blast at the lead capital ship. Every round hit its mark, right at the center of the vessel. The hull quickly started to glow from the amount of energy being forced against it. One of the ships fired a single torpedo that bolted toward the weak spot. It tore through the hull breach and exploded inside the massive vessel. The blast cascaded throughout the ship. Soon it ripped apart from the inside out. Each triangular section broke off and seemingly shattered from the internal blasts without make a sound.

As the massive vessel fell apart, the attacking fleet broke off into two groups. Both groups then fired on the closest enemy vessels to them. The six-point star shaped dreadnaughts were torn apart by the laser blasts of the Spartans, like butter being cut with a hot knife. They peeled apart and ruptured after torpedoes slammed into the breached hulls. The Spartans charged right down the line of vessels letting energized projectiles fly. The small crafts kept close to their motherships as the debris flew at them. One was seemingly heading right for Rose. It stopped when it slammed into her shields and bounced harmlessly off. None of the Claw ships seemed to be able to react in time as their vessels fell prey to the onslaught. Behind the rampaging Spartans was a trail of destruction. The broken Claw ships drifted as they burned in the vacuum of space.

Once the attackers reached the end of the Claw formation, the Spartans headed right toward the space station. It's not like there was any real opposition left to stop them. In seconds, hundreds of torpedoes rammed the station sending whole sections flying off into space. Every round was concentrated at the center. The sphere vanished in a ball of fire with the two metal pyramids rocketing off from the force of the blast. Both started to plummet down towards the planet. The Spartan ships veered off and left the orbit of the doomed world. Behind them, the two pyramids turned red as the fragments dropped lower and lower into the atmosphere.

The attackers reformed into their V-shaped formation and headed for another world in the same system. This one was next to a Slip Gate. It was in the shape of a massive halo with pyramids at four points of the ring. The alien world looked almost identical to the last one, save the two giant artificial meteors dropping down on top of it. There were two flashes of light as the objects hit the surface. The once illuminated city vanished seconds after the impact. A dark cloud rose up sending chills down the spins of the pilots as the ashes covered the hemisphere. Zara asked, "What the hell did we just do?"

Holly came over the comm, "All transports, preside to the planet codenamed 'Eagle's Stable.' Make landfall as soon as possible and destroy everything you see. Draw out the elites and kill them. That's your only task. Don't jack it up!"

"We're decoys. Aren't we?" Hank pointed out the painfully apparent situation. Valery grumbled in dismay, "Never thought the Spartans would throw their own comrades under the bus."

"Well the Claw seem to have no problem with being buddy fuckers. Why would our government be different?" Alan said in disgust.

"So much for trust," Calvin told him as half of the Spartan battle groups veered off towards the red colored Slip Gate. From the planet's surface came a swarm of fighters flying right toward them. There were also a dozen triangular Claw frigates desperately trying to protect what was left of their world. The destroyers fired in unison, taking out the frigates with ease. All of them were relentlessly hit with weapons fire until the fatal hit was struck. The ship would go still for the briefest second before dropping back down to the planet. Some of the transports opened their doors to fire massive warheads at the world below. The projectiles rocketed towards the surface and turned whole cities into mushroom clouds in a single hit. All their transports started to rock violently and glow red and blue as they made their descent into the atmosphere. The destroyers all backed off and stayed in high orbit. Pushed to the limit, the energy shields and armor kept their occupants from burning up. There seemed to be several thousand transports all coming down on the world like a meteor shower. Each ship had a long glowing tail behind them. Everything got brighter as they got closer to their landing zones. The sky turned purple, and the surface became more defined.

Calvin took a long look at the city they were dropping down on. It was a set of several mega-structures that rose as tall as mountains. They were in a circular formation around a massive cone-shaped structure that was made of what looked like white stone. The ground in between them seemed to be covered in glass. The cameras adjusted to the light that reflected up at them. It was like looking at a glass hedgehog with marble spikes. Without warning, hundreds of projectiles flew up at them trying to slow down their assault. Alan laughed, "Wish we could get high right now. One hell of a light show."

"We're fucking augmented! We physically can't get high!" Rose pointed out. Valery joked, "Shit. No after party then?"

One of the transports next to them was directly hit and ripped apart in the air. Calvin ordered, "Tighten the formation up! Focus on the fucking task at hand!"

The others hesitated for a second. Calvin shouted again, "We need to combine our shields if we don't want to get blown out of the fucking sky! Now tighten up!"

They got closer to him and merged their shields together. Several rounds prematurely exploded in front of them. The flashes of light and smoke almost blinded the team. Suddenly all of them lost control of their Crain transports as their boosters slowed their descent. The HUD showed them the words, "Dust off."

Their Mechs were thrown out into the open as the Transports flew back up into space. The Titans used their boosters to adjust themselves as they dropped. Rose shouted, "How the hell are we supposed to operate these fucking things again?"

"Just think about it! Literally... or would it be figurative?" Calvin told her as he swung his Titan's legs down and used his boosters to alter his course. The others followed suit. Alan scoffed, "No one cares about grammar! Anyway, we should deploy decoys and smoke bombs, but what do I know? I'm not in charge!"

"I'm stealing your idea and passing it off as my own," Calvin mockingly told him as Valery laughed, "Spoken like a boss!"

"Don't call me that!" All of them released small grenades that either created holo images of their Mechs or dispersed smoke to camouflage them. Another warning appeared in Calvin's HUD. Valery shouted, "Easy grammar fascist. Enemy contact!"

Calvin looked over the horizon and saw a fleet of Claw fighters and transports coming at them. They stayed close together combining their shields to protect themselves from orbital pot shots. Calvin ordered, "Let's get close, then open up on them with everything we got!"

"How about we pick them off from afar, you know, reach out and touch them? That's the whole point of projectile weapons," Rose suggested sarcastically. Calvin aimed his weapons and replied, "Good idea. Oh, look out for that anti-air fire."

"What anti-air?" Zara huffed. She was suddenly hit multiple times. Her Mech's shields went down and her limbs were torn off. A plasma round went up the machine's torso and exited though its head. "That anti-air!"

"Little late with the warnings, aren't we?" Zara snapped at him. The five of them fired back at the turrets and tanks below. It took multiple shots before they were destroyed. Their bubble-like shields had to pop before they were truly vulnerable. Hank blasted everything apart indiscriminately. The rounds took out whole sections of the glass roof as it caved down into the structure below it. The glass shattered so loudly, they could hear it through the massive Titan armor. All of them started pushing their boosters as they got close to touching down on the surface. Calvin told Hank, "Don't overdo it with your boosters. You'll burn them out!"

"Yeah right," he huffed in defiance. They got close to the artificial ground. Calvin, Rose, Valery and Alan landed safely. Hank came down like a rock and crashed through the glass covered surface below him. He lifted one of his Mech's arms with a thumbs up, "I'm okay!"

Suddenly, a rocket and multiple plasma shells flew into the breach, exploding Hank's Mech. The surface they were standing on started to crack underneath them. It didn't help that hover tanks were also taking potshots at them. Rose charged the tanks head on and fired every weapon she had, only stopping because of the recoil. Multiple tanks were blown apart from the barrage she sent out. Calvin shouted at her, "Don't rush forward, moron!"

Before she could react, several laser rounds came from underneath the surface. Her Titan lurched forward, crashing into the glass and shattering it. Rose screamed as her Mech was ripped in two. Two Claw Mechs rose from the underground. They were jet-black, save the white heads, and resembled the aliens that made them. Their torsos were just a round cylinder. Their limbs, on the other hand made up most of the machine, going from their shoulders all the way down to their hand-like feet. "Have either one of you two taken on a Claw in combat?" Calvin asked.

"Sort of," Alan and Valery responded. Both Claw Mechs charged at them, running across the glass surface like dogs in a sprint. Calvin shouted, "Use proximity rounds. Pay attention to the air!"

Alan aimed his weapons up at the sky and fired blindly. Suddenly one of the Mech appeared before him rattled with burning bullet holes. It slammed downright in front of him and went through the glass leaving a trail of smoke. He laughed, "That was easy!"

Calvin quickly shouted, "Get away from that Mech! Double tap!"

The Claw Mech reached up and wrapped its limbs around Alan's machine. Franticly, he jabbed the butt-stock of his cannon into the machine's head. It was too late. The explosion took Alan out. His Titan went flying backwards losing its limbs and slamming against a skyscraper before dropping against the surface. Meanwhile, Calvin and Valery were firing away at the other two Mechs. One dropped underneath the surface. The other threw two grenades. Calvin quickly lobbed a countermeasure grenade in the air. It sent enough shrapnel forward to cause both explosives to harmlessly go off prematurely. Valery shouted, "Boost!"

Both went up into the air as one of the Claw Mechs crashed through the glass-like surface while firing up at them. They fired back. The machine was able to get out of the way by curling up into a ball and rapidly rolling forward. The other machine leaped into the air and boosted towards them. It sent out multiple holo decoys. The one on the surface sprung up and aimed both weapons at them. They glowed as they were about to fire. Calvin suddenly grabbed Valery and activated a stealth drive and a holo decoy. Together they dropped down at the last second just as the real Claw Mech swung at them with its plasma knives narrowly missing their torsos. The other machine fired and accidently hit his friend. Its body detonated, and head flew into the air in flames. Calvin and Valery fired at the lone Mech enemy once they hit the surface and before it could react. It ripped apart from the inside and vanished into smoke. Valery cheered, "Nice!"

"Fuck yeah it was! We got this!" Calvin shouted in triumph. Valery tapped his shoulder, "Up!"

Several hundred Claw Mechs were being dropped on top of them. Both Valery and Calvin fired everything they had up in the sky. The machines banded together combining shields. Rounds just bounced off them. A group of Claw Mechs popped out from behind the formation and fired. The Titans took several hits before they ultimately went down. The surface below them crumbled and they fell to the underground. Calvin looked up as his machine let out sparks and smoke. In the sky, he could see others Mechs engaging in battle. His view got obstructed when one Mech looked right down at him as he haplessly laid in the rubble. Calvin lifted his machine's left hand in the air and gave the enemy the middle finger, "Bang!"

The machine fired at his cockpit.

Chapter 2
Regroup
Date Unknown
S.I.S. (Spartan Interstellar Ship) Leonidas
Mess Decks

CALVIN was the first to wake up. He sat up on a blue padded bench and looked at his surroundings. He saw his other four squad mates also waking up. Hank and Alan both looked like Calvin. Alan had darker skin, green eyes, and curly blond hair. Hank was pale with brown eyes and black straight hair. Zara, Rose and Valery also mirrored each other with minor differences. Valery had lightly tanned skin, blue eyes, and a mix of blond and brown hair. Rose had red hair, green eyes, and pale skin. Zara had black hair, gold eyes, and dark skin. Zara screamed, "What the hell is going on? We just fucking died!"

"What? None of you have been killed before?" Calvin asked with surprise in his voice. The others looked at him with puzzled expressions on their faces. Alan scoffed, "Why am I not surprised that you've been killed before, Cal?"

"Long story, Al. And what that's supposed to mean, fucker? I lasted longer than you did!" Calvin snapped at him as Hank got up, moving his body around. He franticly checked himself to make sure everything was still attached. Zara yelled, "How are you okay with dying again? Also, how are you still alive? How the hell are we still alive?"

"I got better. Like I said, it's a long story," Calvin told them, annoyed by the fact that he was being used again. Alan scoffed at him again, "Don't give us that crap! Apparently, we got the time! Just give us the abridged version."

"Okay. Short version: I got used. I helped overthrow the Alliance. I was an Alliance operative all along and didn't know it. I fucked the Vegans' shit up, too. Had split personality disorder with a dead Spartan by the name of Alec Dumont. He's an asshole. I caused the Spartans to take over the system... no more Alliance. Short enough for you all?" he explained to them as Rose laughed, "Cool story, Cal."

"Fuck you, Rose!" he shouted at her while giving her the middle finger. Rose kept laughing at him, "You're so fucking gullible!"

"You aren't? How the hell did you end up here then?" Calvin asked as he leaned back in his seat. She didn't say anything for several seconds. He grumbled, "For crying out loud, please tell me you all don't have amnesia, too."

"Who said we had amnesia? Why did you leave that part out, Cal? That kind of seemed important to the story," Zara inquired. Calvin reached up and rubbed the top of his head, "Thought I implied it when I said I didn't know I was a fucking operative all along."

"Sure, you're not just a loon? You had a split personality disorder, nut-job." Alan mocked him. Calvin shouted at him, "It's more complicated than that, asshole!

"Yeah, calm down. Now you mentioned something about time travel? Also, I think Holly said some bullshit about a Deus ex Machina, right?" Valery asked as she was trying to add things together in her head. Calvin huffed, "She told me I was a freak... also that I could manipulate time and shit. They're vague."

Rose shouted, "Is anyone else wondering why the hell we're working for the Spartans? I mean I could have sworn that I warned the Alliance about those terrorists before they could do any real damage. At least that's how I remember things happening. Sort of..."

"Your memories could be lies... they were with

me." Calvin told her feeling regret at his actions, "What does everyone else remember? Anything useful?"

Hank went next, "I thought I got memory loss from getting shot. Well, the Alliance was able to hold Mars but lost half the system to the Spartans. When that happened, both the alien benefactors joined in causing the destruction of our system. Guessing that's not how things turned out here?"

"That's some shit. Thought things were bleak for us," Alan went on, "My friends and I managed to take out a Spartan Team and steal their identities just as they won the war. I think that douche Dumont was one of them. Say what you will, but when the ship is going down, sometimes one must put on a dress to get on a life boat. Worked out... I think." He looked around, still confused as he felt his body for wounds. Zara told them, "All your stories sound very familiar. I thought the Spartans and Alliance came to a truce. Any idea on why we remember things differently?"

"For all we know our memories are fake. Maybe we're from alternate timelines," Valery speculated quietly. Calvin sighed, "Could be either or. Got any other memories you want to share, however fake or contradictory they may be? Just nothing boot camp related."

"Fuck you! I never go full boot! Well, I got augmented after New Nexus because of a dirty android...

don't ask. After that I helped the ship I was on to escape. That didn't do us any good because our tech was painfully inferior to the Spartans. Our ship got shot down and we made a last stand at Olympus Mons. Managed to escape and capture an armored suit of theirs. With that we managed to use it as a Trojan Horse to take over a Spartan ship. That led us to our victory over the Spartans. Last thing I remember is the battle of the Slip Gate. Our ambush was hastily put together. It was sloppy to say the least. I managed to kill off an entire Spartan team by myself..." Valery paused thinking about what happened, "...then a Claw smashed my head."

Calvin's eyes widened, "I think you got my old memories! That or your life happened to mirror mine closely." Everyone looked back at him. "Okay, you've all told me your stories. I'll go more in detail with mine. I was you..." Calvin pointed over to Valery. Alan laughed at him, "Had some work done, I see."

Calvin huffed, "Shit! Set myself up for that one. Moving on. As far as I know I've always been a man! Wait..." He paused as Alan started laughing. Zara shouted, "Stop making this so damned awkward!"

"It's not me that's doing it. Just pointing it out!" Alan told her as he giggled to himself. Calvin spoke loudly, "Moving on again! What happened to Valery sounds exactly like what I believe happened to me." Calvin looked at Alan as he laughed. "Well, I ended up with memory loss after that Claw smashed my head in. Think I told you how I thought I was a Spartan operative. We managed to set off an EMP burst that set our system back to the Stone Age, the Vegans, too. The Claw got to have their expansion though. Right?"

"After this, their people will be motivated to take the galaxy. Do you think that Deus ex Machina has something to do with time travel? What about timeline jumping?" Valery asked him.

"First things last, how the hell are we still alive after getting killed?" Hank asked in a traumatized voice. Rose grumbled, "Resurrection? Could be as simple as a copy and paste. Something dies, make a new one of them!"

"That sounds disturbingly plausible. So why..." Alan was about to ask when Rose barked, "No more fucking questions! I'm getting a damned drink!"

"You're putting your thirst ahead of figuring out important information?" Zara asked her. Rose replied with the middle finger.

"To top that off, you're technically an artificial being! You don't need to drink, Rose!" Hank told her. She huffed, "Well apparently I was programmed with taste, and I'm going to use it, Hanky!"

She got a drink of carbonated sugar water and started chugging it down. "Wait a second, if we're artificial beings, then where would the liquid go after..." Rose got cut off by Valery, "Bodily functions aren't a priority right now! Figuring out how we got into this mess is, not to mention, trying to get out of it."

"You're not a priority now," Alan told her. "Valery replied, "Oh shut up! You're breaking my ovaries!"

"What? Thought they'd be used to the abuse?" he told her with a smirk. She kicked him in the crotch. He dropped to the deck, crying in pain. Calvin and Hank both gasped in shock. "Shit!"

"Nice to see we're wired just like our organic makers. Is every alternate version of me an asshole?" Valery asked them while Alan still moaned.

"Look who's talking, sucker punching people in the crotch," Zara scoffed at her before taking another swig of her drink. Calvin rubbed his head harder in frustration, "We're getting side tracked. I mean, how do I know whose timeline this is or if everything we know is a lie?"

"That Claw mentioned something about you killing Yosemite. Kind of narrows things down a bit," Hank replied. Alan shouted while still in pain, "So we can blame you for this!"

"Fuck off! I'm not taking the blame yet." he told them while looking up at the overhead. "Well, there's one bright side to all of this."

"Besides the explosions?" Rose asked him. He moved his head back to where it was level again and shrugged, "We're ass kickers! Isn't that cool?"

"More like ass kicked." Zara shouted at him. Calvin moved his arms up when he saw his wrist. It read *1A*. "Any of you all have this on your wrists?" he queried the team.

They all looked and found the same thing. They watched each other as a light started to flash in the room. "Guess we should keep that number low," Zara whispered.

CHAPTER 3
SECOND DROP
DATE UNKNOWN
ORBIT OF EAGLE'S STABLE
CRAIN TRANSPORT

CALVIN opened his eyes and found himself back inside the cockpit of a Titan Mech. He was reentering the atmosphere along with the other five members of the team. Next to them were transports jettisoning more Mechs to the battle blow. The meteor shower of Crains and other types of transports looked familiar. Above, the fleet was blasting apart Claw vessels that were entering through the Slip Gate. They were getting torn apart piecemeal style. Their debris would end up falling to the planet and burning up next to the descending transports. Soon the sky changed from black to purple as they came right on top of the Claw's air fleet. Again, all the Titans were ejected from their transports and sent flying through the air. Zara shouted, "Why couldn't this just be a bad dream?"

"You're a bad dream!" Alan told her as they used

their boosters to stabilize themselves in midflight. Calvin quickly ordered, "Take out the small fries first, then the bigger bastards!" The six of them opened fire at once. The small triangular Claw fighters took multiple hits before they would go down. The transports were able to fire back at them. They managed to dodge the laser blasts quickly and land on top of a massive transport with a hard thud.

Their machines left dents in the hull as they slammed into the vessel. Hank landed hard enough to break the transport in half. He boosted off the craft as it plummeted back down towards the planet. Zara caught him and pulled him onto the transport she was on. Several of the Claw fighters came up to engage them. They managed to fly sideways and fire back at the same time. Alan took out a whole squadron with his shoulder mounted cannon. They fired in rapid succession, and every round hit its mark. One round halved a Claw transport. Metal flew out, disintegrating the craft. Calvin ordered, "Form up into groups of two! Stand back to back and take out those fighters as they come!"

"Too late!" Rose shouted at him. Each of the transports started doing barrel rolls. Calvin quickly boosted upwards as the craft rolled over. His machine stood on the narrow edge of the craft. A set of fighters fired plasma rounds from beneath. He quickly had his Titan leap off of the transport as the rockets impacted into the hull. Calvin had his Titan boost forward and grab onto one of the fighters. The weight of the Mech pulled the craft downwards. With the Mech's free arm he aimed and fired taking down the other fighters with his handheld cannon. The recoil of the weapon made his machine vibrate as the rounds exploded next to the fighters, covering them in shards of molten metal. They'd soon plummet out of the sky trailing black smoke behind them.

Another transport fired at Calvin. He pulled the fighter down and used it as a shield for the rounds. The Titan fired the leg mounted grenades at the transport. A lucky couple rounds went into an opening on the craft and it exploded from the inside out. Calvin boosted himself forward and used the falling transport to leap upwards. As he went up, the transport below him went down in flames. Valery reached down and pulled him up onto her platform. It was rocking from side to side trying to buck them off. Rose went to where the cockpit was in the transport and stabbed the area with a plasma knife. She caused the craft to spin out of control. Rose boosted off just as the two ships crumpled into one another, sending sparks and metal into the air. Zara and Alan were back to back on one of the transports firing at the fighters as they came up. Hank leapfrogged from fighter to fighter, destroying one with each step. All the transports suddenly clustered together. They almost made a solid platform. The whole unit got together in a circle. Valery asked, "Any ideas on what they're doing?"

"Sending in their own Mech," Calvin guessed correctly. From the sides of the transports came multiple Claw machines. Alan laughed, "They have us surrounded; they don't have a chance."

"Fuck yeah!" Calvin cheered as the six of them fired at once. The Claw Mechs did the same. The Titans merged their shields together, forming a protective shell as the enemy machines shot at them. The transport fired off shrapnel rounds up into the air that came right back down on top of the group. The shield got smaller and smaller with every hit. The Claw Mechs banded together and charged forward. Calvin shouted, "When I give the order, we boost up in the air, blow a hole into the transport, then fly through it!"

Right after he said that, ten Claw machines leaped into the air and poised themselves to fire. "Now!" he called.

All six of them rocketed up into the air, dodging the Claw's plasma rounds, and blasted a hole inside the transport. They then dropped back down through the hole as the machines charged at them. All six of them passed right through the burning craft, leaving grenades behind.

The whole formation went up in a massive cascading blast. While falling out of the sky, the Titans used their boosters sparingly to slow their descent. The team saw other groups of aircraft being taken down in the distance and fire fights on the ground. Again, they came under fire from below. Alan got hit multiple times and his Mech was torn apart. The other five quickly aimed up and fired back at the Claw machines. Calvin yelled, "Hell, fire at everything!"

They did. All their mounted weapons went off sending every round they had into anything that was in their sights. They concentrated fire on the weakened machines, taking them out in a hail storm. Rose shouted, "Incoming!"

The surface suddenly seemed to come up at them. They activated their boosters and used the momentum to fly across the surface. The glass structure below them cracked as they flew above it. One of the Claw Mechs suddenly appeared and landed right on top of Rose, impaling her machine with its long arm. They vanished into the underground as they were enveloped in a plume of black smoke. A warning flashed in Calvin's HUD. He quickly flipped over and fired downwards as a Claw Mech leaped up through the thick glass. The shields on the machine popped and he got direct hits in on the torso. Zara suddenly got pulled down into the underground.

Hank yelled, "Not again!"

"Just take as many of those assholes down as you can!" Calvin yelled as more of the Claw machines leaped up in front of them. Valery and Calvin managed to stop a few. Hank went all the way forward getting impaled multiple times with plasma knives. His Titan was thrown aside and fell through the glass. Valery sighed, "Just you and me again."

"Let's make it count." The two of them ditched all the weapons attached to their arms, legs, shoulders and back to lighten their loads. They pulled out their external weapons. Calvin and Valery were surrounded by five enemy Mech, three in the front and two in the back. "I go up; you go below?" he asked.

"I was hoping it would be the other way around!" she told him jokingly. Calvin laughed, "From one creep to another, you're being creepy."

"You're the one with your mind in the gutter!" she snapped back at him defensively. Before he could respond, one of the Claw Mech jumped into the air as the rest of them opened fire. Valery went down through the glass, and Calvin went up in the air. He did a flip over the enemy Mech and shot it in the back at point blank range. It went down in a violent crash and burst into shards. Valery came up underneath one, stabbing it in the chest while shooting the second machine simultaneously. That machine managed to deflect the rounds away. She boosted back to the surface, the dead machine falling backwards into the hole. Calvin shot at the two other Mechs as he flew towards them. One took cover in the underground structure as its partner got struck with a grenade. The upper half of the machine vanished in a flash. There was a shower of glass covering the last Claw Mech as it fell flat on its back. It rose up taking a swipe at Calvin with its glowing talons. Both Calvin's external weapons were destroyed.

Valery had similar issues. Both her projectile weapons were ripped from her mechanical hands. She pulled out a second set of plasma knives and locked blades with her opponent. Acting quickly, she blocked a stick from the glowing claws with her plasma knives. The two machines leaped side to side while dodging each other's jabs at one another. Calvin and Valery both braced themselves as the two Claw Mechs swung all four limbs in a single swipe. Both Titans blocked the arms while moving their feet out of the way of the swiping talons. "Get close to me and we'll switch targets!" Calvin called out.

"Right!" Valery agreed. Both boosted closer to one another. They flew backwards as enemies kept trying to stab them. Once they were almost back to back, they spun around and stabbed each of their respective enemies in the torso. The force of the stab sent both enemy Mech flying backwards. Their torsos burst open upon impact with the ground. Valery cheered, "We did it!"

Suddenly in cooperation they got stabbed through and through multiple times. The other Claw machines seemed to have come out of nowhere. Both collapsed as their machines started to burn from the damage. Calvin gasped as his body was ripped open. Blue fluid leaked all over the cockpit. He was shocked by how fake his internal organs were. "Damn it... this is getting old."

He suddenly saw the Claw get taken out with direct hits to their torsos and heads. Another group of six Titans came charging at them. One of the friendly machines paused for a second looking into the breach in Calvin's Titan. The pilot seemed to be looking right at him. He gave a wave, "Kill these fuckers!"

Calvin's body went limp as everything faded to black.

CHAPTER 4
INDIFFERENT
DATE UNKNOWN
S.I.S. LEONIDAS
BERTHING ONE

CALVIN woke to the sound of screaming. "That was fucking bullshit!"

He sat up on a green cushioned couch. The others were noticeably traumatized from their deaths. Calvin pulled down the sleeve on his coveralls and checked his arm. *2A* was branded into his skin. They were all in a berthing lounge. All of them sat up on the fixed chairs and couches. Red lights illuminated the room. Rose joked, "Look, your favorite lighting!"

"Remind you of your old job?" Alan asked her. Zara shouted, "What the flying hell is going on? We just died again! Why are we in a different location?"

"Like we have the answers!" Alan replied sarcastically. Hank stood up annoyed, "Leave her alone, asshole! We've all been through too much crap. Stop acting like a prick!"

"Pull the one out from your ass first!" Alan told him bluntly. This set Hank off and he started swinging his fists at Alan. He laughed, "Rape!"

Then he got hit in the crotch, "You cheap bastard! You're going to die again…again!"

Alan kicked Hank into the bulkhead as he got up. Valery stepped in between the two of them, "Enough! Are you all fucking professionals or are you just damned juvenile delinquents?"

Calvin laughed as he stretched out on the couch, "Really? That line? Please! We're not even real! We're fake! Why worry about professionalism anyway?"

"Speak for yourself, asshole." said Rose angrily, enraged at the whole situation. Calvin told her sarcastically, "How dare you talk to your team leader like that!"

Valery snapped at him, "Maybe we could try to find ways to not get killed instead of bullshitting? You know, figure out how to deal with this situation instead of being a pack of douche bags."

"Deal? We're dead anyway! We're not meant to survive this operation! Now would you kindly let me enjoy what free time I have left? Fight amongst yourselves for all I care. Just leave me alone," He told them while stretching out. Alan nodded, "You heard the man!"

Both he and Hank started hitting each other repeatedly. Valery got out of the way, holding her hands up in defeat. Both were hitting hard enough that blue liquid started to come out of their wounds. Zara shouted, "Why the fuck are they bleeding blue?"

Both Hank and Alan stopped throwing punches and stumbled back from another. They looked down at their blue soaked coveralls and noted, "That is damned peculiar."

"Hey, Team Leader! What is this?" Rose asked with frustration in her voice. He snapped in raged, "Fuckers, I don't know already! I'm just going to take a stab in the dark and say that we're not humans anymore. Hasn't that fact sunk in already, dipshits?"

"No! I don't want to be a machine!" Zara shouted in despair. Hank shouted, "This is fucking bullshit!"

"Wait a second. Are we even who we think we are?" Rose asked. Valery shouted, "Oh no! Don't you dare go off and have a fucking existential crisis now of all times!"

"Why would we have a problem with affirming our existence?" Hank asked while relocating his nose. Alan grumbled, "Really moron? I must have hit you harder than I thought. Think about it! We're fucking copies!"

"This is all your fault, fucker!" Zara snapped at

Calvin with anger and sadness in her voice. He was busy rubbing himself against the couch. "Don't go using me as a scapegoat. I didn't cause shit!"

"You're an uncaring bastard! That's all you have to say after you dragged us into this shit!" Rose shouted at him as she was shaking in her green coveralls. Calvin grit his teeth together and stood up letting out all his pent-up frustration, "Fuck you all! I'm not the one who dragged you into this! I got dragged into this crap just like all of you did!"

Alan laughed, "Oh yes, shrug off your responsibilities of leadership when you're supposed to be in charge. Fucking boss!"

Calvin took a couple steps forward and roared, "Don't you fucking dare pull that bullshit on me! Also, don't call me a boss! You can be in fucking charge for all I care! All this crap has been beyond my damned control! Bust my balls and wonder why the hell none of you jerks are getting *my* understanding! I was afraid of the day I'd see myself become an asshole. Now I see myself turning into multiple assholes all at once!"

Rose shouted, "Fuck you, too, douche! People screwed you over. Does that give you the right to be an ass to others? Can you blame us if we're a little on edge after dying twice and finding out we're just copies of other people? Not to mention, we have no idea how we got here. Give us a break."

"Oh, so you all can be assholes then? It's fine if you fuckers bust my balls and use me as an emotional punching bag, but if I lash out, it's wrong? None of you fuckers have shit on me when it comes to dealing with jacked up revelations!" He pointed out as he took a couple steps towards them with clinched fists. He wanted to throw a punch so much, but he held back.

"Once again, jackass, you're in fucking charge! Like it or not. Also, revelations? We're copies and possibly not in our right timelines anymore! Hell, those memories could just be lies! That's on top of the fact we're being used as cannon fodder again! Don't act like you've got a monopoly on pain!" Hank yelled at him. Calvin laughed as his fist started to pop from the strain of being clinched, "Then don't try forcing your fucking problems on me you are a condescending bastard!"

"Condescending? Fuck you! We didn't ask you to become our leader! Maybe I should take charge! You sure as hell suck at it you cry baby!" Hank shouted taking a couple steps when Valery got in the way, "Please, everyone, chill the flying hell out!"

"Wow. How politely aggressive," Alan smirked. Calvin got an ever-better idea and went up to the door and looked up at a camera, "Next bastard that gets on my case, I'm going to start telling Holly that she's just like her maker, maybe even pester her with questions! She loves questions; doesn't she?"

"You wouldn't…" Rose was about to call him out when Zara punched her across the face, "Shut up!"

"You like it rough?" Alan laughed. Both Rose and Zara punched him in the face. "Totally worth it!" he moaned.

"Enough, you damned drama queens! How about we all give each other some space! Okay?" Valery suggested trying to keep her temper in check. The others sighed in reluctant agreement. "Fine! Sounds good to me," Hank sighed as he walked off. Rose started wandering around, "I'm going to see if anyone has anything worth stealing."

"Happy time," said Alan as he went into the head. "Assholes!" Zara shouted and walked off down into the berthing area grumbling to herself in disgust. Calvin went back to the couch and let out a long sigh as he got comfortable again. Valery went over to him, "Damn. We got issues. Not easy looking in a mirror; is it? Pardon the ball busting in advance, but act like a fucking leader already."

"Mirror?" Calvin calmed down. "It's more like watching a film play repeatedly. They said the exact same things that others did, always blaming me for everything. And they aren't completely wrong, Val."

"Cal, fuck your pity party! Like we said, you're not the only one that got lied to, and cut yourself some slack. How were you supposed to know any different?" she asked while standing near him. He looked up at her, "I should have known something was up the way everyone was acting around me. I was too stupid and gullible to add things up until it was too late."

"Well you could blame the way you're programmed for how you acted. Your brain was jacked up at the time. Wasn't it?" She told him. He laughed, "Never thought I'd be thankful for being defective for once. Sorry I was being an asshole, Val."

"I've been called worse, Cal. It was kind of jacked up you used the 'C' word," she told him. He looked up at her in confusion. "Condescending," she revealed.

"Oh. I feel guilty about that one. That was a bit harsh," he went back down and closed his eyes. She asked him, "Might sound a bit off subject, but have you ever had a real dream?"

"Good question." He realized he couldn't sleep. Valery thought of something, "Do you think our Mechs have an ejection system?"

He sat up, "Why didn't I think of bailing out

earlier?"

"It's kind of blasphemy to eject. Then again, sometimes it's better to live to fight another day. We might last a little longer if we can survive our Mechs being trashed," she suggested with a reassuring smile. Calvin nodded in agreement, "Sounds good and dirty all at the same time."

"Don't get attached to your machine. They're going to get wrecked. Sorry to bring up work. I just want to live a little longer this time," she told him innocently.

"Don't we all? If you have any other ideas, let me know. I'll steal them and take all the credit," he told her with a wink. She laughed, "Spoken like a true boss."

"Bag of Saggy Shit?" he asked. She told him, "Big Oblivious Stupid Sod."

"That's a good one," he laughed. She joined him on the couch. Calvin was no longer red and had calmed down some more. Valery leaned forward and asked, "So I guess you've dealt with things coming back and biting you in the ass. Right?"

"That apparent? I really hate being so easy to read. Makes me think I'm boring. Hope you're not," he leaned up slightly and adjusted his head to where he could easily see Valery. The red light illuminated her. She told him, "I try to be as entertaining as possible. Remember, we might have different organs, chromosomes, and memories, but we're still the same person… sort of."

Calvin smiled to himself at the thought of something. "Memories? Did you get in trouble for a drunk dial?"

"Thought you didn't remember anything before all this started?" she asked trying to dodge the question. He told her, "I was just making up a story. Now you got to tell me what this is about. Unless it's too touchy of a subject."

She looked up into the overhead thinking. The red lights illuminating the room making her eyes shimmer. "I don't even know if these things really happened," she began. "Well, what I remember is that I was dumb enough to make a drunk dial once. It was calling a Chief Price. That guy blue falconed me, not to mention he was a total prick."

"Buddy fucked?" Calvin asked smiling. She explained, "More like head hunting. He fed me a bunch of bullshit. It was just crap to get me to lower my guard. Then he screwed me over. He was always aggravating to talk to, and thanks to that douche, we had to spend a four-day weekend in the bridge. When I got out, I got drunk. That only made things worse, but at least I got transferred soon after." Before Calvin could ask, Valery told him, "I never really got over it. My dreams got crushed and I was stuck.

Kind of thankful I'm here now. Might be a nightmare, but at least I can be that wannabe I always wanted to be."

"When did you make that dial if you don't mind me asking?" Calvin wondered as he sat up straight, interested in what she had to say. For once their conversation wasn't about work. She nodded, "After I got out of the brig and was talking to my family members who gave me the inspiration to tell him off. Backfired to say the least."

"Thought we'd be orphans," Calvin said with surprise in his voice. Valery wondered, "Technically we are, but why would you think we'd be orphans?"

"Most operatives are orphans, right?" he asked innocently enough. She pointed while giggling, "Maybe our makers wanted us to have happy memories to keep us going during the shit they get us into. Besides, we're not heroes, just survivors."

"In your memories, did you have any other family?" Calvin asked gleefully. "Don't know. Like trying to remember a dream" she told him. He decided not to ask about her mother, probably best he leave that alone. Instead he asked, "Go on any good vacations?"

"Several. Might have gotten on each other's nerves, but we had a good time. Does it matter if it really happened or not, Cal?" She asked him to ponder the thought for herself.

"Depends on your perspective. What ever happened to that 'blue falcon' that screwed you over?" he wondered. She told him with glee, "He was onboard a carrier called the Excelsior. It went down over Mars. All hands lost. As much as I won't miss him, I'm not going to revel in his death at the expense of others, though I'd like to think he was crushed to bits at the end."

"You're petty. Also, I think that might have happened in my timeline, too," he said not knowing what to feel about it. She nodded, "No point in being butt hurt over memories that may or may not have ever happened. So back to the task at hand, how are we going to survive longer the next time?"

"Longer?"

"I don't think the next time will be the last. Nothing ever ends quickly. One of the ideas I have is to link up with the other units. We're going in piecemeal right now. It's not helping. Plus, I think we need to get a clearer objective on what we're doing. Hate to say it, but we need to ask Holly a few things."

"You'd think we'd be allowed to plan this out better. Does it matter? We're eventually going to get whipped out and used as an excuse for the Claw to expand their territory," Calvin stated grimly. Valery leaned forward and placed a hand on his shoulder, "Fuck that! There is always a way out! Not saying die yet! The only way out is through. Also, you need to work on winning over the others. I feel like I'm spitting out too many platitudes."

Calvin looked down while grumbling, "Kind of. Well, I really don't think I'm leadership material. Do you want to take charge?"

"You were picked to lead. You're going to rise to the occasion. That and I don't want to," she assured him. He nodded, sitting upright with his legs on the deck, and paused, "Would you mind if I just want to enjoy this moment of quiet right now?"

"Are you comfortable with sharing the silence?" she asked leaning back. "Let's see." He saw a remote on the table and activated a holo show that showed stars' systems drifting in the dimly light room. One by one the others joined in and started watching. No one really spoke or paid attention to how long they were staring. They lost track of time and let what imagination they had allow them to feel like they were flying through the cosmos. It seemed to end all too soon. The main lights came on almost blinding them. Holly's voice boomed on the intercom, "Time to go."

Everyone sighed in dread. Calvin got up and

begrudgingly asked, "Holly, please... could you give us some more details on what we're supposed to do? I know you said storm the capital, but how exactly? Also, is everyone else from alternate timelines or something?"

"Everyone besides you is a copy from someone from an alternate timeline. You're hallucinating right now while you get dropped back down on the planet to give you all a break from being killed. Now, head to the main capital building, and kill everyone there. That will draw out the elites. You'll know them when they come out. Kill them immediately when they do. Good luck."

"Wait a second! What about..." There was another flash of light, and each of them dropped to the deck, still and drifting in and out of consciousness.

CHAPTER 5
GRIND
DATE UNKNOWN
EAGLE'S STABLE
CAPITAL CITY

THEY were already on the ground in their Mechs when Calvin came to. The battle raged around them. The sky rained down with debris and disintegrating vehicles. The scraps burned as they came down. The larger shards crashed into the building, cracking the glass. The artificial surface that seemed to stretch over the city was covered in broken glass, and there seemed to be constant fireworks show going on in the sky. Bombs and flashes of light never seemed to stop. Plumes of smoke rose from the city after all the damage it had taken.

Calvin looked over to his side. A friendly unit was getting wiped out. Quickly, all six of them charged over to help. They managed to land several hits on the enemy Mechs before they could react. The damaged machines collapsed onto the metal ground rattling with burning bullet holes and in flames. The remaining Claw Mechs ducked into a hole and fired from their concealment. All six Titans lay down on the ground, firing back from the prone position. One of the enemy machines took a hit right in its round metal head, lifting its body up enough to expose its torso. More rounds impacted the machine, leaving a hole. Hank took advantage and threw a grenade inside, exploding the enemy. A warning came across Calvin's eyes. He quickly rolled over and shot a Claw Mech as it came down on top of him. He boosted out of the way as the machine crashed into the ground. Calvin saw several more of the Mechs coming down on top of them, "Incoming!"

The others rolled over and fired up into the air. One of the destroyed machines landed right on top of Hank causing him, Alan and Rose to fall into the underground area. The other three were able to boost away before they got caught up in the cave in. The ground cracked, the rupture stretching all the way to one of the massive skyscrapers. The glass sail-shaped structure tipped over towards the crack in the ground. Massive shards of glass rained down on top of them. "Shields!"

The three of them got together and threw shield grenades all around. Then, they fired up into the air cutting down the shards of transparent metal. The building toppled over towards them. It gave out a violent screech as it came down. Calvin ordered, "Fire everything into the building and we'll fly through!"

Each of them aimed their walking arsenal at the structure. They sent so many explosives into the building it split in half. "Fly!"

The remaining team members boosted off the ground and up toward the breaking point of the building. To be nimbler, they shed the extra armor and weapons, dodging the metal shards as they rained down. They made it through to the other side just as the building shattered against the surface. Dust, ash and shards of glass flew into the air. Valery shouted, "Look out!"

They dropped out of the air and into the dust cloud as seven Claw Mechs flew at them, firing away. Each of them pulled out an external plasma cannon and returned fire, managing to take one out before they were enveloped into the cloud. They boosted at the last second and gently touched down on the surface. The three of them backed into each other, forming a protective triangle. Their machines had a hard time seeing through the dust and smoke no matter which spectrum they used. Alan's voice suddenly chirped, "We're still alive!"

"That's great! We'll talk more about it after we die," Calvin responded grimly. Zara huffed, "How optimistic."

Rose shouted, "We're not the only ones down here!"

"Don't be so vague!" Hank shouted at her. Calvin checked his sensors and was warned that there was movement nearby. He could see the vibrations on the ground. "When I give the word, boost again. Roger?"

"Got it," The other two responded. They didn't have to wait long. The vibration on the ground increased rapidly as the enemy charged them. "Now!"

They boosted up into the air leaving behind grenades as three enemy Mechs lunged where they were just standing. In the ensuing blast, the machines flew backwards. The other three Claw ambushed them while they hovered in the air. All the Mechs fired at once. Calvin managed to dodge the round that came at him by boosting downwards and scored a killing blow, the rounds flying through the machine's torso. The other two weren't so lucky. Both Valery and Zara got shot down. They managed to bail out before their suits crashed and burned into the ground, taking a machine down with them. The last Mech in the group cut the plasma cannon in Calvin's mechanical arms. He used the remaining grenade and threw it at the enemy. The explosive ripped its upper torso off its legs and sent it flying backwards through the air.

Calvin franticly looked around him realizing he was the last in his squad again. He had two internal arm mounted cannons pop out as he aimed them from side to side. He still had his chest, head, and stomach mounted weapons as well. In both the mechanical arms he grabbed giant plasma knives. He poised his Titan, ready be attacked. The dust cloud around him cleared. Calvin was surrounded by a dozen enemy machines. All of them had their arms pointed at him. Their built-in cannons started to glow as they fired up. Calvin sighed, "Shit."

Suddenly, five of the Claw machines were taken out. The other seven got distracted long enough for Calvin to drop a holo decoy and fly at the closest two. He rapidly fired, hitting them repeatedly. Once their shields popped, Calvin ducked down behind them and stabbed them both to make sure they were neutralized. He used the damaged machines as shields as three fired at him. The remaining two were destroyed in a massive volley of fire. Five friendly Titans came up to him, "Thanks, guys. I owe you one."

"Calvin?" all of them said in shock. They sounded exactly like his teammates. He suddenly got on the comm, "Guys, where are you?"

"We could ask you the same thing," Valery responded over the comm. Alan laughed, "Now you see what we're talking about. We're not the only ones down here. Get it?"

The other Alan spoke again, "Hey! Who's that poser you're talking to?"

"Someone call me a…" Calvin cut him off, "Who are you all?"

"Your squad dipshit," the other Rose told him bluntly. The other Zara asked in a panic, "How can he be our leader when Calvin just got blown to bits?"

"I think we all know the answer to that question," Calvin sighed thinking about it for a second. The other Hank answered, "We knew we were replicates before. Just didn't think they made a shit load of us."

"We're all in this together. Might as well fight that way, too." Calvin said, and he motioned them to follow him. The other Rose asked, "Where are we going?"

"Strength in numbers. More of us, less times we get killed!" He shouted as they rushed to assist another squad that was in distress. One Titan got knocked down onto its back. The enemy Mech was about to stab down with its talons. Calvin quickly boosted over and stabbed the machine right in the torso and head with his plasma knives. The downed Titan quickly joined in and finished the machine. It rolled over and grabbed a plasma cannon and shot a Claw Mech that was wresting with one of his squad mates. The machine was knocked off the Titan. The

Titan got back up and stabbed the enemy with a plasma knife. The rest of the Claw fell back under fire from the *others* behind the destroyed skyscraper. The surviving squad members got up as Calvin got on the comm, "Good to go?"

He suddenly heard his own voice, "I think. I am hearing voices after all."

"Don't sweat it. We've got assholes to kill," he told himself. A different Valery asked, "This is going to get confusing really quickly! How are we supposed to tell each other apart?"

A message came to him over the comm from his team's Valery, "I think we can tell one another apart by the numbers and letters on our wrists. Check them."

Calvin remembered seeing *2A* tattooed on his wrists. He went back to his suit's vision and suddenly saw several more enemy Mechs boosting over the destroyed skyscraper. The code name Thins popped up in front of his eyes. Seemed fitting. Everyone dropped to whatever cover they could find and fired at them. From behind the Spartans, other friendly units joined in on the fight. The Claw Mechs dropped out of the sky like raindrops. The only one that made it through the wall of fire, came right down on Calvin. Calvin tried to fire, but his weapons had overheated and couldn't fire. He dropped his cannon and pulled out both plasma knives. Right as the enemy landed, he swiped upwards cutting the machine's arms off but not before it impaled Calvin. Calvin stabbed his knives down. Sparks flew from the machine as he shoved the glowing blades in deep enough to kill the pilot. The enemy Mech stopped moving and went backwards onto the metal ground, lifeless. Calvin 2A dropped to the ground, too, in his Titan. One of the others rushed up to him. Everything was fading in and out. He shouted, "Band together!"

"I think I'll do something similar!" He opened the cockpit of his Titan and rolled out of the damaged machine. An aid kit dropped on top of him. He quickly scrambled to patch himself up. He injected himself with multiple rejuvenators and put on liquid clotting agents to patch the holes inside his chest. He'd just got done putting patches on his armored suit when he looked down at the glass surface he was sitting on top off. Massive cracks were forming. "Shit!"

The glass gave way and he plummeted down below. His boosters slowed him down enough that the glass hit the bottom first. It made a loud shattering sound that echoed in the tight space. Calvin landed behind a fallen pillar and took cover. He pulled a rifle off his back and peeked over his shoulder. He saw the sun shining down through the breaches caused by the firefights. A

Thin's leg came crashing down near him. Calvin leaped out of the way as it slammed into the concrete surface. He looked back, seeing a massive black mark on the ground where the Thin's hand landed. There were several small fires burning and trash was all over the place. There seemed to be flickering holographic advertisements playing in the background. They were so distorted he couldn't tell what they were supposed to be. He turned around, sweeping his rifle across the store. It looked to be filled with toys. There were dolls of Claw females and action heroes, but he couldn't decipher the writing on the boxes. Calvin suddenly heard an electronic noise emanate next to him. He swung his rifle towards the noise and pointed his weapons at a small Claw. "A kid?" he asked surprised.

The child seemed to be pointing a toy gun at him and pulling the trigger. He looked different from the other Claw he'd seen. This one only had one joint per limb, two wide eyes and flat teeth. He still had the same spiked hair and long fingers and toes. The Claw child's mother came up and grabbed him. She wasn't as tall as the other Claw he'd dealt with. The mother seemed to be pleading with him not to shoot. Calvin made the motion with his hands to leave, and the two of them quickly ran off around the corner. He heard them talking to others.

Calvin threw a proximity grenade right at the edge of the store and moved backward. Out of the corner of his sight, he saw a Claw operative about to kick down a door. Calvin swung his rifle and fired. The rounds went through the flimsy wood and knocked down the operative. He threw a grenade in there to make sure he wasn't going to get back up. The other explosive went off when a soldier tried rounding the corner. Calvin went through the smoke and started to run away. He ended up right in front of a whole platoon of operatives. He quickly went forward and stabbed the first Claw in the head while shooting the second two with his rifle. He pushed forward on the dead operative and held down the trigger to his weapons, firing blindly. He almost stumbled on several bodies as he moved along. Calvin was suddenly hit in the side, knocking him down. He aimed his arm mounted pistols and fired at one of the Claw. Calvin got up feeling like his whole left side was on fire. A grenade flew over his head and landed right behind him. He quickly boosted away, but not before the grenade exploded, sending him flying forward. Calvin was caught out in the open and quickly got hit with plasma fire. He fired back with his weapons. The Claw took one to the head and went down for good. Calvin had multiple wounds on his torso. He let out a long moan as he got back up. Parts of his armor fell off and his helmet no longer functioned. He pulled it off seeing one more Claw operative leap at him. He got stabbed in his right arm and in the torso. Calvin kicked the soldier away with his right leg and shot him in the head multiple times. He bent down in pain as he heard a click next to him. He aimed his pistol to the side seeing the kid again. His mother was screaming at him as he aimed at Calvin. Calvin gave a smile and tapped his forehead with two fingers, "Live a little longer."

His head suddenly went backward as a hole burned through it. He went flat on his side looking up at the kid as his mother took him away. She gasped in horror as she saw he still had a smile on his face as he slipped away.

CHAPTER 6
DATE NO LONGER RELEVANT
S.I.S. LEONIDAS
READY ISSUE MAGAZINE

CALVIN rose up from the nonskid deck and checked his wrists. It now said *3A* on it. He huffed, "At least we're still Alphas. I really don't want to see this number get any bigger."

"I don't think any of us have the luxury of that," Valery told him. The other five were sitting around next to stock piles of weapons and machinery ordinances that would go to the transports, Mechs and fighters. All the rounds were secured in racks that could be lifted in and out to the hanger deck. Half the ordinance was already gone. The overhead had several sprinkler heads and the bulkheads were painted white. The racks themselves were all non-spark producing metal. The door was latched shut and locked from the outside. Calvin held his head, "I'm really starting to have second thoughts about what we're doing. I mean I just ran into a kid. Bastard might have shot me dead, but still."

"Oh, a poor hapless child is the thing that's causing you to have second thoughts? Not the fact we're being used by assholes to start a war for expiation?" Rose asked him bitterly with her eyes twitching in frustration.

Valery told him, "Hate to rub salt in the wound, but it's too fucking late to have second thoughts now. We're all in!"

Zara mentioned, "Well maybe they'll get the hint and throw in the towel so no one else gets hurt?"

Alan laughed and sarcastically told her, "Oh yeah, I'm sure they're going to let us walk after we just killed millions if not billions of them. I totally see a truce in our future! Also, anyone else wondering why Holly would put us in here with all the explosives? Not to mention, why would they put our spare bodies here of all places? You think they have all of us on standby for when they're ready for us to go again?"

"She just wants us out of the way until it's time to send us off to die. Are you honestly thinking of setting a bomb off in here?" Rose asked him. Calvin asked, "Wait a second. When did you all get wasted again?"

"You really ask the wrong questions a lot," Valery told him.

"It was after you for once, loser," Alan smiled.

"Hank got blown up by a rocket launcher, Zara got shot in the head, Valery got stabbed, Rose was crushed under a falling level and… that's it."

"You got killed by stepping on a mine. And I believe your counterpart warned you about it before you stepped on it. Way to listen to yourself buddy!" Valery rubbed it in with a smile. Calvin asked, "So all of you are number 3A?"

"Again, poor choice in questions," Alan told him as he checked his wrists and grumbled to himself. The others looked down at their wrists and nodded. Calvin thought to himself, "Guess we all come back at the same time. Besides our counterparts, what else did you all find down in the underground?"

They all looked silently forward, not wanting to answer the question. Rose broke the silence and started off quietly, "Death."

"Figured as much. This is a battle. There's going to be death," Calvin said unable to keep his sarcasm back. Zara told him, "She's talking about the civilians. Turns out they used the underground as a refuge. It didn't work. Everything fell in on top of them during the battle. You'll get your chance to see it soon enough."

"Damn. I feel like an asshole." Calvin said to himself with guilt. Alan nodded, "At least you know what you are."

"You're just a big a douche, too. Not like we killed any of them…" He paused as Valery stared at him coldly. "Only thing we can do is try to last longer. I mean we're getting organized now. That's something."

Valery spoke up, "I don't think any of us signed on to commit mass murder! Maybe we should find a way to rebel or get the hell out of this system, something other than just following orders blindly."

"As much as I'd like to rebel, we'll only last ten seconds out in the galaxy before we're either killed for treason or tortured to death for our crimes. We're fucking stuck," Calvin pointed out to her. Hank cried, "This is fucking bullshit!"

"Just now figuring that out, slow motherfucker?" Alan mocked him. Hank shouted back, "Fuck you!"

Alan scoffed, "You would, wouldn't you? Hell, now you can fulfill your lifelong dream of fucking yourself, literally!"

"You know what, asshole. If I wanted to fuck myself, I would bend you over! Besides, I don't need sex. Holly seems to be fucking us all the time anyway," Hank replied. Alan nodded, "Not bad. One of these days you'll have a good comeback."

"If I wanted a comeback, I'd get it from your

mother," Hank told him. Alan laughed, "You do know we might have the same mother, sicko."

"A fucking birthing tank is our mother!" He shouted in dismay. Zara patted him on the back, "Valiant effort, Hank."

"You unfocused douche bags! Do none of you care that we might get thrown back to our deaths again?" Rose shouted at them. Calvin rocked his head side to side thinking, "We're getting better. Aren't we?"

"She's right. There's always a way to get out of a shitty creek! Didn't our asshole Doctor say something about Deus ex Machina? I know we brought the damn subject up. Don't drop it this time!"

"Maybe it was crap to keep us from rebelling. Even telling us those words just gives us false hope." Alan told her with a smile. Zara asked, "Isn't most hope false anyway?"

"Fucking pessimists! Just going to roll over and take it?" she snapped, growing more frustrated by everyone's acceptance of the situation.

"Why worry about the inimitable? This is a suicide mission after all," Rose pointed out. Valery snapped, "This isn't right! I don't want to be sacrificial meat!"

"It's what we were made for, literally for once, to be disposable. Get over it," Alan told her trying not to laugh at her anger. She shouted, "No fuckers! We shouldn't have to accept this crap!"

"Could be worse." Zara told her. Valery replied, "I fucking hate that phrase! I mean being sent off to die and being remembered as a war criminal isn't bad enough?"

"We could be used as sex slaves by perverted bastards that make us eat unclean food and…" Zara got cut off when both Hank and Rose shouted, "Stop!"

Alan laughed, "Someone knows the Aristocrats joke! Wouldn't take you as someone with a demented imagination."

"You never asked," she told him. Calvin sighed, "At least we know it could be worse."

"Settling for being bullet sponges shouldn't be an acceptable upgrade," Valery exclaimed, letting her frustration come out. Hank pointed out, "Not rock bottom though."

"Fuck settling! How could any of you all be fine with ending every mission in a body bag? How about we say no for once? I'm not just going to keep flying into the fray with no way out!" Valery punched the bulkhead hard enough to leave a dent. "What more can that douche Doctor do to us anyway?"

"Sell us off as sex dolls for…" Zara started as Rose laughed, "We get it! Wouldn't put it past her."

"Don't give her any ideas!" Hank shouted.

"Well, maybe we could at least ask a question. She won't send us off for that. Wait a second, we shouldn't even be property," Calvin thought aloud. Alan looked up, "Seeing how we're literally made for this… we kind of are… that's crap."

"We're not property!" Valery shouted. Calvin spoke up again, "Hell, being an asshole sounds better than this speculative bullshit. Wish Holly didn't have mommy and daddy issues, not to mention a couple of loose screws in her head."

Rose's eyes went wide as she looked up and saw a camera looking down at them. She gasped, "I think she… shit!"

"Fuck. Do you know if she can hear us?" Calvin asked. The camera moved slightly as Holly's voice came over the intercom, "I can hear you. I think I could make some major currency off you all on the black market. You'd be shocked at what some perverts are into."

"Shit," Rose said with fear in her voice. Valery got up, "Fuck you, Holly! You're stuck in this shit storm with us, so maybe you should be more open to actually trying not to be an asshole and just maybe we'll survive the next mission."

Holly started laughing bitterly. The others looked

at each other in dismay and fear. Calvin asked, "Are you laughing because there's no way out of this?" Valery spoke up, "There is a way out of this isn't there! Tell us, fucker!"

"No, not with that attitude of yours. Look, like I said earlier; I'm working on getting us all mulligans as we speak. Leave it at that," she told them with dread in her voice. The others looked up at the camera with wide eyes wondering what she was talking about. Calvin spoke up, "I have a question. Why are we waking up in different places in our hallucinations?"

"Keeps your minds on their feet so to speak. There are only so many places on this vessel to hang out. Also, trust me when I say you all don't want to constantly pop up in the resection labs," she told them plainly. Rose asked, "Why couldn't you just tell us that from the start instead of being so touchy?" She didn't reply. "Oh, very mature!" Rose said annoyed.

Calvin sighed, "Got something out of her at least. Anyone else have bullshit stories they want to swap in the meantime?"

They all looked at him in dismay. "Let's not spend time wondering about the next drop. Our imaginations can go to some fucked up places," he paused looking at Zara as she shrugged. "The last thing I remember is we started linking up with other versions of ourselves and

75

pushing forward. Was that still going on when you all got wasted?"

"Yeah. We had a beachhead going down there... in a manner of speaking," Hank told him. Calvin nodded as Zara shouted unexpectedly, "I'm tired of being a number!"

Valery pattered her on the shoulder, "I know, right. How about we rebel?"

"Like I said, it wouldn't last long. We've always been outnumbered in one way or another. We'll find a way out of it when the time comes. Okay?" Calvin told her trying to be diplomatic. Zara rolled her eyes, "This is fucking bullshit!"

"Cal, I'm starting to agree with her. We should totally go anarchy!" Alan laughed. Valery wanted to punch him as Zara asked, "How can you just be okay with this? I mean none of you thought of a way to get out of this crap?"

"Hello? Were you even listening to me, or were you too busy coming up with your own version of the Aristocrats?" Valery asked her. Zara sighed, "I thought it would have been funny."

"You're not going to be a comedian, Zara. Don't quit your day job," Alan told her bluntly.

"Val, you keep talking about a rebellion. Do you even have any ideas on how we can get out of this? Wishful thinking isn't going to work. You say we *should* rebel. But the question is, can we? Anyone know anything about reprogramming? Unless you do, as crappy as it sounds, I don't see us having much freewill. Top that off, Holly said she's working on getting us out of this creek we're in," Calvin told her. She had nothing and looked down in defeat, "Probably just trying to save her own ass. I really thought you had an idea. So back to the underground we go. Do you all think there's a way to sneak through the tunnel system?"

Alan replied, "Don't think so. The whole city from top to bottom is packed full of Claw soldiers. We haven't even run into the so-called elites we're supposed to take out."

Rose huffed, "Please Al. How would you know who's an operator?"

"If they were already here, we'd be dead quicker," said Calvin. He saw he had an implant under his skin on his right arm. He started tapping it and a holo image of the Claw city popped up in front of them. It showed the ongoing battle raging below. Valery spoke up, "How the hell are we not being affected by the space battle?"

Calvin showed her the outside images of space. The Spartan fleet was guarding the Slip Gate and had complete control of the area around the planet they orbited. "Okay. Why don't we just blow up that damned gate?" Val pondered.

"Don't you remember? This is a suicide mission. We're all supposed to die. Or were you too busy daydreaming about pulling a rebellion you can never do in real life, Val?" Rose told her with a condescending smile to hide her fear. "At least I don't suck at life like you do, Rose," Val retorted.

"Enough!" Calvin shouted. "Our only job is to draw out their elites. Either the fleet is doing a good job blockading the gate, or the Claw are mustering up everything they have to throw at us."

"No shit, detective," Zara mocked him. Hank grumbled, "What does any of this matter? We're all going to die again anyway. That's what we're here for. Isn't it?"

Zara broke down and sat on the deck contemplating her mortality, "Fuck this! There has to be a way we can change our fate, right?"

"Deus ex Machina again? And stop saying that we're going to die. Fuck that!" Valery shouted.

"Think Holly would be kind enough to explain it?" Calvin thought out loud, "Well, in the meantime, back to the unimportant matter of doing a better job on the next drop. How about next time, we make it to the capital building this time." He brought back the image of the battle at hand. The Spartan forces seemed to be making headway to the massive structure. It looked like two giant glass hands holding a giant silver sphere. Valery pointed out, "How about we drop on top of that building to save time? We got a beachhead after all."

"That sounds suicidal," Rose said. Calvin told her, "We get it! How about we stop beating the dead house about how screwed we are? Damn. Focusing on real priorities, we'll use the Titans as battering rams and have them boost all the way down. At the last minute, eject and let them crash into the structure. Wait a second. We might have to deal with an energy shield, too."

"We may be able to get data from the troops already down there to modify our shielding, so we can pass through the barriers. Once we do, we'll only have our armor to keep us alive from when we enter to the time we get into the building," Valery suggested. Calvin smiled at her idea, "Sounds good. Any other suggestions?"

"How about we threaten to blow up this ship if we don't pull out now?" Hank told them. Zara laughed, "Like they'd let you do that. Try to do something with one of the explosives and see what happens."

He punched at one of them, and his hand hit a force field, "Motherfucker!"

"Moving on. You do know that while we bullshit

up here, our counterparts are getting wasted down there," Alan pointed at the images of the battle below. A whole squad of six just got wiped out by a single blast. The fighting got more intense the closer they got to the capital building. Most of the Claw forces fell back to that building and formed a formidable makeshift bulwark around the structure. Calvin motioned to the camera, "If you want to have us go down there right now hero, then just annoy Holly some more. Be my guest, Al."

Alan got up when Hank stopped him, "Say one word and you're dead the minute we're planet side."

"Don't you think that's just a bit extreme, Hank?" Alan asked nervously. He laughed to lighten the mood and patted him on the shoulder, "No. Castration would be extreme. Never shoot anyone in the crotch... unless it's personal."

"At least you're not an unethical genital shooter," Calvin complimented jokingly. Hank nodded, "Have to have a line somewhere."

Rose shouted in frustration at the camera, "Hey fucker! Are we going back or what?"

"If you insist," Holly answered everyone looked at Rose, "Shit. I didn't think that would work."

"Good going, slick," everyone told her just before they felt the familiar piercing shock.

CHAPTER 7
INTO THE BREACH
EAGLE'S STABLE
CAPITAL CITY
TITAN COCKPIT

CALVIN felt the familiar feeling of free fall. There were bursts of smoke around him as the anti-air fired up at him. As he got lower, he saw several of the massive skyscrapers that were now flat on the ground with black clouds rising from their twisted remains. The entire artificial surface of the city was covered in cracks, black craters and debris from destroyed ships and vehicles. The rest of the Spartan forces surrounded the massive capital building in a circle. They used what they could to build cover for themselves and slowly pushed forward. Both sides blindly fired at each other across the no man's land. The massive shield was slowly shrinking from each hit it sustained. The dome of energy made a flash with every impact it took. It was like looking into a lightning storm. Anything that tried to go into the open was torn apart by the weapons fire.

Calvin quickly glanced to his side and saw several others next to him trying to attack from the air as well. Guess great minds think alike. They came down like rockets with their Mech's boosters firing up as they came down on top of the building. All of them fired off all their decoys into the air as they got closer. The anti-air only got thicker the further they descended. Once they got to the shield itself, they lost control of their Titans. They went spinning around in the air uncontrollably, being peppered with rounds. The machine flew apart from the flack. The machines' severed body parts flew sending sparks and smoke trailing behind them. Almost every machine that penetrated the shield was a sitting duck soon after. Multiple squadrons of Titans were blown apart instantly after passing the barrier.

Calvin's squadron passed through and his machine started to act up. The controls weren't working, and the machine took multiple hits. Knowing he was doomed, he waited until the last second before ejecting. Calvin went flat against his seat as the doors few open and he rocketed from his disintegrating Mech. He gasped helplessly as he headed right for the capital building. Quickly, he curled up into a ball as he slammed into the edge of the roof. His armored suit left a dent where he impacted. He stretched his body out as it recovered from the shock. Calvin started to slip downward and quickly boosted himself up and onto the roof. He rushed toward the first opening he could find. A couple auto turrets and Claw soldiers opened fire on him. He kicked up a large metal fragment and used it as a shield. It got hot to the touch with the rounds flying into the shard. It worked long enough for him to get to a set of doors. He slammed his body into them as hard as he could and went flying through the opening. Multiple rounds burst through the destroyed doors, just missing him by a hair.

Calvin fell onto his face right in front of a whole platoon of Claw operatives. All of them had on black armored suits with clear silver spherical helmets. Their limbs were if their bodies with two joints per limb. They each stood at least eight feet tall. They aimed their weapons at Calvin and fired. He quickly threw a flash bang in the air and leaped forward. When it went off, it blinded them long enough for Calvin to jump over a ledge and fall down the brightly lit stairway. He landed on the next floor with several more Claw soldiers quickly aiming their rifles at him. He leaped back into the center of the stairway as they fired. Calvin used the boosters on his suit and moved his body, swinging it from side to side to keep dropping floor after floor. The operatives closed in, trying to shoot him at each passing floor. They poked their heads over the ledge and fired down at him. Calvin aimed his shoulder mounted cannon and fired up at the ceiling. The blast sent a rain of shrapnel and fragments downward. Multiple operatives lost their heads, the rounds blowing them apart. It looked like an egg getting smashed. Their bones and brains came down on top of him as he struggled to get further down into the building.

He dropped through the stairwell with his full weight, crushing the limbs and head of anyone he fell on top of. There were violent crunching sounds and screams filled the air as he did so. Calvin got stabbed in the back on the way down. He spun around and blindly fired his arm mounted weapons downward at the next floor that would come up. That kept the operatives from getting a clear shot at him. He started to get sluggish and got stuck on a couple of the ledges but used his brute strength to bust his way through. Using his suit as a battering ram had its drawbacks as his body and armor were quickly getting worn out from the impacts. Calvin then accidentally went into one of the rails with his legs on both sides, his crotch slamming down onto the metal. "Ah!" he screamed. Despite armor and augmentation, he still felt pain. Even the Claw operatives paused for a second out of sympathy. Calvin threw two grenades before rolling back into the center of the stairway. His face mask slammed into the next set of railing, disorienting him for a second. Calvin spun around as he helplessly hit every ledge on the way down. His body slammed into the floor with a loud thud. Dozens of grenades came down on top of him.

In a panic, Calvin quickly rolled away. His body went flying through another set of doors as fire and shrapnel followed him. He ended up crashing right into three Claw operatives. He rolled over and set his cannon to overload and dropped it on top of them. Calvin boosted himself up, rushed forward to the next group. He swung both his fists forward and punched one of the aliens in the torso, crushing his ribcage and armor alike. Grabbing onto the wounded operative, he used him as a shield while the other Claw took potshots at him. He went straight for the elevator and crashed through the doors just as his cannon exploded. The building rocked from the blast. He just managed to avoid the flames as he plummeted down the elevator shaft. Calvin tried to stop himself as he saw a lift coming straight up at him. He boosted out of way, crashing through another set of doors just as the lift flew past him. "That was close," he thought.

Instinctively, Calvin activated a shield grenade as he came under heavy fire again. He went back into the elevator shaft as flames rose up toward him. The shield lasted long enough for him to pass the fire unharmed. Above him, several Claws leaped down firing grenade rounds. He moved the shield generator up as it took the impact. Calvin started to approach the bottom of the shaft as he got lower. He aimed his knees and legs downward and fired every grenade and rocket that was strapped to him. He activated another shield generator as he went through the breach, losing his pursuers. He was again in a brightly lit area with more operatives rushing him. Calvin dropped a holo decoy and boosted upward along the ceiling over the Claws. He blindly fired at them, not worrying about aim at this point. He got stabbed in the torso again when one of the operatives lunged a bayonet at him. Despite the wound, he kept going. His HUD started pointing him down the hallway. He followed it like a dog would follow a car. Words popped up in front of him that translated to *generators*.

He followed the hallway as quickly as he could. He pushed his boosters to the max, weaving around the tight spaces with the Claw just around every corner. As quickly as they appeared, all of them started to back away from him. He didn't care why they were running from him. Maybe they were scared. It inflated his ego. Calvin felt invincible as he charged deeper in. He reached a massive door that opened for him. Inside was a huge pillar of glass that contained what looked like a storm of light chasing one another like thunderbolts. All around the room were holo controls and screens showing readings off the generator. The pillar brightly illuminated the room with the clash going on inside. It stretched up and down as far as his artificial eyes could see.

He was about to step inside when he paused for a second. He threw a holo decoy in. Nothing happened. Calvin quickly checked behind him. No one was there. He waited a few seconds and then threw another decoy inside. This time a Claw operative with a golden helmet came crashing down on top of the holo image right in front of Calvin. Both threw grenades at each other and leaped backwards at the same time. From above, another operative dropped down firing proximity rounds at him. Calvin quickly changed directions and went forward, dodging the projectiles. The two grenades in front of him went off at the same time. He used his last shield generator to protect himself. Calvin got a warning and leaped forward just as the airborne operator came down slashing at him. He put all his energy into boosting towards the energy pillar. Calvin dropped his last holo decoys to throw off his attackers. He was just about to reach the pillar when he was knocked out of the air. His head went flying backward after getting an uppercut. Calvin's energy shields went offline as he crashed into the floor. He suddenly came under fire from several locations at once. His HUD flashed over and over showing his armor deteriorating with every hit. Calvin blindly fired at the pillar with each round bouncing off from the shield surrounding it. Both his arm mounted weapons were then blown off. He then took multiple hits to the head. His armor couldn't save him. Calvin went flying backward across the ground and slammed into the wall from the force of the hits. The Claw all threw grenades down at him. Unable to see, he ripped off his destroyed helmet. As his eyes cleared, he saw grenades coming straight for him. The words Deus ex Machina flashed in his mind.

He felt a surge of energy inside as everything slowed down around him while he felt like he was speeding up. It's like he was hit with an adrenaline shot. Calvin went up into the air and started grabbing grenades and throwing them right at the middle of the pillar. He watched as each grenade glowed red as it was about to go off. The grenades hit their mark, blasting through the pillar's shields, exploding at once. He flipped the back mounted rocket launcher on his back and fired a plasma rocket. It flew straight through the breach. Calvin suddenly went limp as a round went through his head. His saw the light escaping through the pillar and into the room, burning everything.

He smiled as his skin melted off.

CHAPTER 8
CHECK UP
DATE UNIMPORTANT
S.I.S. LEONIDAS
INFIRMARY

CALVIN woke up laughing. Alan asked, "So what's the joke? You?"

"No, your performance. You were dead on arrival, and I died after I destroyed the power core, wimp," he laughed. His body somehow felt strong, despite the strain he went though. Valery patted him on the shoulder, "Fuck yeah!"

"Thank you. Some positive reinforcement for once!" Calvin said as he leaned back against the padded table. Holly walked up to him, "I see that you finally were able to use those abilities I've been talking about. Took you all long enough."

"Speaking of abilities, how come I can't go back in time? Thought you said I could? Lastly, is this a hallucination, too?" he asked before saying, "Wait. Never mind. I'll figure it out. Please don't flip out because of my ignorance."

"Oh, chill out. I have bigger things to worry about than you are acting like an asshole," Holly responded plainly while fooling around with her holo-pad. "My counterpart thought Deus ex Machina would be a fitting name for something extraordinary. As for the time travel thing, it hasn't happened yet. Creating alternate possibilities on the other hand, look around and you'll see them. Why do you think you're surrounded by alternate versions of yourself?"

"That figures," Hank mumbled to himself. Zara asked, "So our commands just wanted to get rid of us?"

"I just told you all you're just copies sold for cheap! For what it's worth, where others see waste, I see the unutilized," she told them while nodding trying to assure them.

"Great, we *are* property. So now that the shield generator is down..." Calvin got cut off by Holly as she started to laugh bitterly, "We're up shit creek still! We're all going to get slaughtered by their elite guards. Enjoy your time planet side because next time will probably be your last," she told them as she went over to attend to patients who were wounded. Rose smiled and whispered, "This is bullshit."

"That it is! Fuck us, right? Don't worry, my back up plan might just work. Might..." she laughed to hide her fear and uncertainty.

"So?" Valery started but Holly threw a metal tray at her. "Oh, real mature!"

"We're just supposed to roll over and die planet side? What kind of plan is that?" Calvin asked, not believing things had gone so wrong so quickly. Hank started to cry, "At least we won't get wasted anymore..."

"Shut up!" Alan shouted at him as he started to pull his short hair. Rose asked, "How badly could we be getting our asses... why did I ask?" She gasped as she pulled up the footage of the battle below. He looked up, "These elites you mentioned are kind of hard to kill."

Images of modified enemy Mech appeared. They were taking out dozens of Spartan Titans singlehandedly. Other images of Claw reinforcements appeared, pushing back the Spartan fleet. They were steamrolling the ships to save their home world. Calvin shivered, "Shit..."

"Why can't we just leave?" Zara asked bitterly. Holly laughed, "Not programmed to. One-way trip. Remember?"

"That's totally cheap!" Hank pointed at one Claw Mech that had a golden head. It tore through another set of Titans. It was suddenly taken down by four Spartan machines stabbing it at once. It exploded, taking them all down in the blast. Valery spoke up, "I can't believe I'm saying this, but we need to go back down there."

"What's the rush? We're fucked either way! Really think Deus ex Machina will save us?" Alan asked them as he sat down plotting his fate. Rose sighed, "Got to believe in something, right?"

"I don't think belief out of desperation is true devotion," Calvin said thinking about it. Zara huffed, "How philosophical."

"Well, I got it to work once. Why not twice? Why couldn't we all get it to work for once?" Calvin asked with everyone starting to laugh. They mostly did it to hide their fear. He sighed, "Never mind then. Worth a shot."

"Never say die!" Valery said out loud. Zara said bitterly, "Never say die."

"Never say fucking die," everyone else said in hopeless defiance of their situation. Rose asked, "Got any drugs we can get high on?"

"We're machines! We can't get high on anything!" Zara shouted in dismay. Alan asked, "Can't get high or drunk. Only leaves two other vices that I know of. Which do you want?"

"For crying out loud, don't get kinky," Hank said with disgust in his voice. Zara laughed, "At least we get to go out with our boots on, right?" She gave a pause. Rose pointed out, "Will anyone even care? As far as everyone else is going to know, we're terrorists."

"I'm beginning to think being in a bureaucratic hell wasn't so bad," Hank spoke his mind as Alan patted him on the shoulder, "You say that now."

He nodded his head, "Point taken."

"Fuck it! Let's at least go out in a blaze of glory!" Rose tried to goad them on.

"How did we end up the victims of Blue Falcons... again?" Valery thought aloud.

"Our asshole makers set us up this way. At least we know why we are the way we are, programming!" Calvin said with resentment in his voice. Valery shouted enraged, "They can't keep doing this!"

"They are, and they will," Holly told her bluntly. She started kicking the bulkhead repeatedly, "Bullshit!"

"Quit your crying and suck it up," Alan told her. She went over and punched him in the head, "If getting sent off to die isn't a good reason to get a grip, then what is?"

Calvin looked over at the holographic images of the battle, "Well, this fight isn't ending anytime soon. Who wants to get going?"

None of them said anything as they looked at the carnage unfolding on the projector. Holly removed the holo images and told him, "Look, like I said. There's a chance of us getting out of this. I'm trying to work something out. Until then, I can make accessing your ability easier. Let me do some adjustments. Besides, what do you all have to lose?" She quickly went over and jabbed her syringe into Hank's eye. He screamed, "What the fuck? You could have just put it in my neck!"

"These could be the last moments of my life. Let me enjoy them! Don't be a drag. Also, this will help out later if we're lucky." Holly went over, pulled out the syringe and patched up his eye. "Now you'll last minutes instead of just seconds!"

"What an improvement," Rose said sarcastically as she got stuck with a syringe. "Ouch!" The images of the battle popped back up, and the team saw two V-shaped formations of Titans taking down several Claw Mechs. Calvin looked down at his arms seeing the number 4A on them both. He looked over at Holly, "How many other versions of us are there?"

"There are twenty sets of you, but not too many left now that the enemy seems to be packing our shit in. Oh, and I should warn you, don't get killed too many times. Once you reach your tenth death, you run the risk of insanity. Also, don't let the ship go down. If the ship dies, so do we."

"Now you tell us," Rose sighed. Holly moved around playing with the syringes, "We can only make so many copies and stretch you so thin before things start going wrong. Another curse we can thank our makers for."

"What a pack of pricks!" Alan shouted enraged. Valery yelled as she pulled the needle out of her eye, "We get it. They're bastards! Stop beating that dead horse. Too many of those getting smashed to a pulp! And stop bringing up how fucked we are!"

Holly threw another metal tray at her. Valery caught it and the equipment that was on top of it, too. The doctor gave a satisfied grin, "Good."

She quickly started throwing other things at the rest of the team. Each one of them was able to dodge or catch what she was flinging at them. She smiled widely, "Very good. Now go back down there and try not to die too quickly. It's been fun! Hopefully Plan B works out."

The six of them were knocked out all over again with the familiar shock.

CHAPTER 9
FALL
DATE UNKNOWN
EAGLE'S STABLE
CAPITAL CITY

ONCE more they were in free fall. The city looked like it was in complete ruin now. Every skyscraper was knocked down, and even the artificial structure that they stood on was collapsing with massive sinkholes. The capital building still stood despite the considerable holes blown into it. The Claw operatives were pushing back the Spartans. The ranks were starting to break as orbital fire added to the Claw's advantage. Calvin got on the comm with his squad, "Let's take out as many of these fuckers as we can. Okay?"

"Why not?" Valery responded.

"For a second there I forgot this was a one-way trip," Hank laughed. Valery told him, "To hell with that. Our victory party is going to be epic!"

"Drink, fight, and fuck all night!" Alan cheered.

Calvin smiled at the delusion of survival and hope. There were others descending next to him. All of them at once seemed to boost ahead towards the Claw formations. Calvin shouted, "That's the dream!"

All the airborne Titans fired at once with every projectile weapon they had. Multiple enemy Mechs were hit in the surprise attack. They fell to the ground which shattered on impact. That still didn't make a dent in their numbers. The Claw kept coming. For everyone they shot down, ten seemed to take their place. Leading their charge was the customized elite unit. These were altered machines, so they stood out like sore thumbs. Their gold round heads shimmered with what light was left in the sky. More of them joined the fight adding to the swelling number of Claw machines. They charged forward with the others following them. The Titans were run backward firing back in vain. Calvin and the others hit the ground running as they charged the remaining elite Mechs. Both groups moved toward one another while exchanging salvos of fire. All the Spartan forces stopped and started to fall back as orbital rounds fell around them. One torpedo took out twenty Titans at once. Calvin shouted through the bombardment, "Let's give these fuckers something to remember!"

Valery moved in first and caught one of the Thins

standing still. It stayed long enough for her to score a direct hit. The round hit the Mech's torso sending it backwards and into the ground. Above, three more Thins came at them from the air. One got torn to shreds by weapons fire as the other two boosted downwards. Valery leaped to her left dodging the plasma round and blocked the glowing arm that came swinging at her. Zara boosted up and got into a grappling match with her opponent. Her Titan forced the Thin down onto the ground. It kicked her off. She fired, and the machine rolled out of the way of the rounds. Meanwhile, Hank stabbed his plasma knife furiously into the side of a Thin, sending sparks and a cloud of smoke into the air. He used it as a shield, lifting it up as its limbs dangled. Alan and Rose tag teamed a Thin. Rose kept its attention while Alan managed to get behind it and shoot the machine in the back. Its chest burst open, sending shards of metal and fire everywhere. Calvin was taking on two elites at once. He dropped the armor and weapons attached to his machine's right arm and pulled his plasma knife out while lying down cover fire with the left. He kept one Thin at a distance as much as possible. They kept trying to rush him, but he always gave them the slip. His Titan ducked down as a Thin swung its arms at him and missed. He felt a rush as he swiped his right arm upwards cutting the machine in half vertically.

The remaining machines started boosting themselves back towards the last standing building. The bombardment kept up, raining down more torpedoes on them. The Spartans banded together as they dodged the falling rounds. They just managed to keep one step ahead as the Titans blearily avoided the blasts. The Thins popped back up and opened fire again taking out another dozen Titans. They all dropped onto their backs with sparks flying from the bullet holes punched through them. Calvin was shocked to see how many Mechs had fallen around him. The entire ground seemed to be covered with destroyed machines leaking smoke and sparks. Another Titan patted Calvin on the back. He heard his own voice telling him, "Come on. Let's get these fuckers!"

"Sounds good to... us... in this case," he said bewildered by the situation. They kept firing, but their efforts didn't seem to put a dent in the Claw's advance. The sky soon was filled with Claw ships appearing ominously overhead and dropping more reinforcements. A torpedo flew down and ripped another twenty Titans in half. The Thins charged again firing everything they had. Multiple squadrons of Titans went down in the onslaught. Calvin's team was quickly peppered with energy rounds, popping their shields and blowing off their armor. Calvin moved forward as all the Titans seemed to band together in a last-ditch effort to hold out. The ships stopped firing. There were enough Thins that their victory seemed all but assured. What was left of the Titan squadrons was stuck in a circle. They combined their shields to keep from being wiped out by the oncoming rounds. Calvin laughed angrily as he fired back, "Never say die..." A tear ran down his cheek as he braced himself for the end. Suddenly Holly's voice came over the comm, "Cease fire! Cease fire! Plan B is a go!"

"What?" In a split second everything went quiet, and the Claw forces seemed to stand down their assault. All Spartans stopped firing, too. "What the actual fuck?" Alan asked in disbelief. Rose shouted, "This is too fucking good to be true!"

"Deus ex Machina?" Hank wondered looking around. Valery quickly asked, "Holly, I know you hate questions and all..." She paused shaking in her machine as everything got eerily still. Holly shouted in a panic, "Transports are on their way. We're getting the hell out of here ASAP!"

"What?" Everyone said confused and worried if they were being lured into a trap. From above, several hundred transports came down. Some were clearly Claw operated. Calvin got on the comm, "Holly, what the hell is going on?"

"Just follow the truce! No damned time to explain right now! Just get on the transports and get back to the ship!" She screamed at him with terror and relief in her voice. One transport came right over head, one per machine. He boosted up and docked inside of the triangular shaped craft. It quickly pointed up to the sky and started boosting upwards. Down below, the other Titans were being loaded up. The Claw was even evacuating strangely enough. There was a planet wide exodus. The amassed Claw fleet was now in full retreat, passing the Spartan ships as they recovered their personnel. There seemed to be millions of different transports flying around and swarming their motherships, all of them trying to get away from an impending doom. Hank asked with terror in his voice, "Why is everyone running? They had us cornered."

"There must be something bad down there if they were willing to let us go to escape." Valery speculated. It didn't take long before the team was onboard the Leonidas. The bay was a hive of activity as multiple transports all landed at once. Some of them were being thrown back out into space because of a lack of room inside. Calvin climbed out of his Titan and then out of the transport. The gravity was deactivated, and the air was off. Everyone had on air tight armored suits as they worked on the Crains that landed. The other five walked up to him as soon as they were onboard. "So, any ideas on what's going on?"

"No clue. Your guess is as good as mine," Calvin told them as one of the crewmen passed by and told them, "Get out of the way! There's an area for you operators to hang out. This isn't it."

"Easy! No need to be a douche," Alan told him. As the six of them walked away from the disgruntled crewman, they saw thirty-six other operatives. Each of them had on a different face mask. Some were of human skulls; others were of animal skulls, regular human faces, or just a plain metal surface with or without eyes. One of them asked, "So, what's your name, letter, number and/or symbol?"

"I'm not a letter or a number! Maybe a symbol though," Alan said smugly. The guy laughed, "You must be an Alan. You're the reason I have to go by Damon now."

"Who cares? Why are we suddenly running away? I mean we were in the gun sights of the Claw, and by some miracle everyone is running. What the fuck?"

"Maybe we gave peace a chance?" a woman pondered. "Oh, my name is Beth. I wanted to be unique in some way. Who am I kidding?"

"Was no one listening to what I just said? This is

way too good to be true. Why are we suddenly getting let go from the slaughter? Something bad must have happened," Zara panicked.

"Yeah, that is kind of odd." Damon said. Hank shouted. "Kind of? What's this Plan B Holly mentioned?"

"Peace?" Beth asked with a smile. Zara snapped, "No! As much as I want to think that, our luck is not that good! There must be something much worse on the way if the Claw were willing to let us go!"

Calvin raised his hands, "Can we all just take a couple minutes to enjoy the fact that we're not dead?"

"For how long?" Beth asked. Suddenly the ship went completely dark and everyone slammed against the bulkhead.

Chapter 10
Date Unknown
Change
S.I.S. Leonidas
Hanger Bay

"WHAT the fuck?" kept echoing in the hanger repeatedly as panic spread across the bay. All the lights were still off with none of the emergency backups coming on. Somehow the gravity was still functional as no one was drifting around. The bay was also pressured and filled with air. Everyone seemed to stumble around in the dark trying to get their bearings. Random people started shouting, "I can't see out of my fucking helmet!"

"My damned night vision isn't working!"

"My body is broken!"

"Who's grabbing my ass?"

Calvin got up after pushing a couple people off him. In his rush to stand upright, he tripped over someone else. Suddenly the person got up and leaped on top of him, head butting him. After the third slamming of helmets together, Calvin punched the person in the chest. He felt relief for only a few seconds before the person was back on top of him and hammering his helmet with clinched fists. Calvin tried to kick the person off as others started yelling in distress, "Get him off of me!"

Soon there were loud shrill screams of agony and the sound of flesh being torn apart. Calvin's face mask got ripped off. He felt air rushing into his suit. Someone lit a flare, and he was finally able to see. To his horror, the person on top of him didn't look normal. Inside its broken helmet was a deformed and mangled face. Its eyes were glossed over white. Blue blood seemed to trickle out of its broken mouth as it growled at him. All its razor-sharp teeth glowed green, and its skin looked pale and rotten. The person had two broken arms leaking out blue fluid yet seemed unaffected by the wounds. It lunged at Calvin. He raised his arms and held the foul-smelling person away from him as it tried to bite him with chattering teeth. He gasped, "Zombies?!"

Several clicks went through the air. "Oh fuck! Our damned weapons aren't working!"

"I beg to differ!" Damon shouted as he walked over to a person being eaten. He used the rifle as a club, smashing the Zombie's skull in with a single quick muzzle strike. It made a popping sound as the bone cracked and the brains splattered. He then smashed his muzzle into the victim's skull, crushing it with his full weight behind the weapon. Blood, brains and bone went all over the nonskid. Calvin grabbed the head of his attacker and started to slam it into the deck repeatedly until the skull broke. He only stopped when the body went stiff. He sat back gasping, "What the fuck?"

"Zombies!" Damon shouted, and he hit the dead's already broken head into smaller pieces to make sure they couldn't get back up. Valery shouted, "We're cybernetics! How could one of us turn into a damned zombie?"

"Cyber Zombie? Cybie…Zomber?" Alan made up some words as fear emanated from his voice. Beth snapped. "We're sticking to fucking Zombies! I don't know why people don't just stick with that word."

"Copyright?" Rose suggested. Zara screamed as Hank jumped on her. His helmet came off showing his jagged teeth and green eyes. She couldn't stop him in time before he came down and took a bite out of her cheek. He pulled the flesh off her face as she screamed in pain. Alan and Valery rushed over and promptly muzzle struck Hank's head multiple times. His head split open and his brains dumped out as his body went flat against the deck. Rose shouted, "What the fuck?"

Valery went over to Zara as she held her wound,

"Sorry, sister."

She quickly jabbed her with her rifle muzzle in the head quick. Zara went limp on the deck as her eyes rolled up into her head. Alan gasped at the sight in disgust. Calvin ordered, "Everyone spread out! Where's the flight crew?"

"Over here!" Someone shouted. Everyone started activating flares illuminating the darkness. They glowed red yet didn't give off any sparks. Calvin and Beth went over to one of the crewmembers. Her back was broken, "Shit!"

"Why couldn't I have been upgraded?" She whimpered from the pain. Valery remembered, "Wait, I thought everyone on this ship was augmented."

"Clones are cheaper than the augmented!" She told them gritting her teeth as she dealt with the pain. Next to her a man was looking around and grunting repeatedly. Damon asked, "What the fuck is up with him?"

Beth walked up to him. "Petty officer, is it? What's wrong?"

The man grunted and looked at her. He screamed in fear and ran right into two of his fellow crewmembers. They all tumbled down to the deck. One of the crewmembers screamed and started fighting with the first one. Beth asked, "What the hell is up their asses?"

As the two crewmembers started fighting each other, one got in between them and tried to calm things down, "Break it up!"

Neither one seemed to understand what he was saying. Valery went up to them, lifted them up by their coveralls, and slammed their heads together, knocking them both out with ease. "This is making the replication shit look normal!"

"Run!" a voice shouted. A woman was running in a full sprint away from another zombie as it ripped off its helmet and let out a high pitched electrical sounding scream. The others rushed over to try to help her when the zombie pushed passed the woman. She paused in disbelief. Valery flipped her rifle around and swung the rifle butt like a club at the zombie's head. It stopped the rifle with its arm, but the arm broke on impact with a loud snap. The zombie didn't care and charged at Valery, trying to bite her neck. Valery quickly pulled out a knife, swung it upwards and cut the zombies head almost in half. The knife wouldn't head up and got stuck in the person's head. Calvin helped her get the knife loose by splitting the head open the rest of the way. The woman walked up to them with a puzzled expression, "What the hell was up with her?"

"She didn't seem interested in you," Damon

pointed out. He looked back at the surviving operators. All of them were slamming their rifles down into the heads of their zombified comrades. They franticly hit them as their heads turned to piles of rotten flesh and shattered bones. Rose went up to them, "I think you got them!"

One of them gave another hit to make sure. Valery shouted, "Everyone, form up into groups! Sweep the hanger for zombies and survivors. If you find any stragglers, send them to gather up by an exit."

"Do you have a plan?" Alan asked as he walked up holding a flare. Calvin told him, "We need to find a way to get this ship working again. First things first, we need to get control of this hanger. Some of us have gone farfel."

"How did this happen? This is fucking weird!" Rose said as she pulled her face mask off. Beth commented, "No shit. At least our suits partly work. For some reason, I can't access any of the systems and my eyes aren't adjusting to the dark."

"Same goes for everyone else here, still mildly functional," Calvin told them as he looked over at the two knocked out crewmen. "Restrain the... grunts. I don't want them doing anything else stupid."

Alan dragged over another two as they kicked and screamed. They didn't even form coherent words while they franticly flailed about. Some more crewmembers came up to them, "We're good! I can talk and shit!"

"Look out behind you!" Valery shouted. Five zombies pushed past them. Alan threw one of his knives right into an oncoming zombie's head. It dropped face first onto the deck with the knife going deeper in and ripping off its jaw. Rose leaped over, grabbed that knife and cut the head off another zombie. Beth and Valery swung their rifles together and squashed the head of another two attackers. Damon kicked a zombie down and smashed her skull with his foot. Calvin jabbed both of his knives into the eye sockets of the last zombie. He kicked the body onto the deck so hard its head split open on impact. Alan asked, "Is it odd to anyone else that the zombies are only going after augmented people and not organics, you know, the humans?"

"This whole thing is jacked up!" Rose snapped in frustration trying to get the blood off her suit. They began hearing *Clear* repeatedly. To everyone's relief, the words *all clear* were spoken.

Calvin sighed, cleaning off his knives, "We can breathe easy for now."

They dragged over the grunts and escorted the organic crewmembers that were still coherent. Everyone was gathered up by the double door airlocks. They sat there holding their flares and rifles tightly. Calvin quickly looked over the group, counting how many operatives were left. "Team leads!" he shouted.

Four other versions of him walked up. Calvin composed himself as best he could, "Okay. Is there are about five squads at four to six strong. We'll have to make do with that. How many crewmembers are still sentient?"

"Only a third of the hanger crew isn't impaired. Half of the organics in general are injured. Don't know about the rest of the ship," said another Calvin. A third Calvin added, "We should get the wounded to medical as soon as possible." A fourth one said, "We also need to get this ship back up and running. Remember, we're still in orbit of a planet and probably falling as we speak. Plus, to add to our shit sandwich, there are other teams onboard. Some of them might have become zombies as well. There are probably other members of the crew that are now dumb as rocks just to top off our pile of crap." He looked down at one of the grunts as he bit at his restraints while hopping up and down. Another team leader spoke up, "What could have caused some cybernetics to turn into zombies and some organics into idiots while not affecting others?"

"There's only one person I can think of who has the answers. She's in medical."

"Who did this to us?" the last team leader spoke up. One suggested, "Vegans?"

"There's no way in hell that the Vegans could have done this. We sent them back to the gunpowder age."

"Isn't it supposed to be Stone Age?" a team lead asked. "That's the closet age I can think of before electricity took off. Besides, they still have technology that would put them ahead of the cavemen." He looked down as one of the grunts rolled around next to him, "Not to mention a lack of elegance."

"It's not the Claw either. I don't think this was supposed to be part of their fall flag operation. I don't think they would have committed to a truce unless they knew what was coming was bad," Calvin suggested.

"You don't say? Who could have put both us and the Claw into the proverbial shit creek? Apparently, they're advanced enough to cripple our ships and castrate our minds."

"Not to mention they're assholes," Valery interjected.

"I think it's been said before. Holly is the only one I can think of who'd have a clue," Alan told them. Rose snapped, "We're wasting time speculating! Like I said, our fucking orbit is decaying. Also, the grunts could be learning how to blow themselves up! Let's move."

"Your point is taken. Another thing, do we have any working projectile weapons? Blunt instruments aren't going to carry us all the way through," Calvin asked his counterparts.

Damon looked down at his rifle, "Maybe we could use the equipment here to jury-rig something."

"Good idea as any." Calvin saw one of the grunts try to run away. The operatives were having a hard time keeping them under control, even with the restraints. One of the operators requested, "When you all find Holly, ask her if she can fix the grunts."

Alan added, "Now when you say fix…"

"Really douche? Who would ever suggest something as fucked up as castration? Don't be an asshole," Rose barked at him.

Damon added, "Wait a tick. Is there a way for us to communicate with each other while moving through the ship, you know, in case something else goes wrong?"

"Like things weren't bad enough already, but point taken. Any ideas?" Calvin asked his copies. One of them piped up, "There's emergency backup communicators throughout the ship. We can check in on them and call other sections of the ship to see how they're doing."

"Great! Let's do that first before we head out. I'll call medical. You call other sections of the ship that might have people in it. Once we're done, we'll meet back up. Cool?"

"How come you get to call medical and get answers first?" One of Calvin's counterparts asked with jealousy in his voice. Everyone looked at him rolling their eyes. "Never mind," he retreated, "Priorities. Sorry to ask."

"Good call. Speaking of priorities, let's get to it." They all went around looking for the communication devices. Beth walked up to Calvin and asked, "Is it cool if we join you? We had to re-kill our squad mates."

"Sure. We had to do the same to two of ours," Calvin said with a hint of sadness in his voice. Alan giggled a bit when Valery asked, "Why are our friends getting killed twice over so funny to you?"

"I wasn't laughing at that. I was laughing because Holly can't do shit to us for asking questions this time!" He smiled as Calvin almost laughed at the thought, "Don't underestimate her."

Both he and Alan went and opened a red and yellow box on the bulkhead. Alan got there first and pulled the headpiece to his ear. He saw the numbers up top and dialed the one he needed. "Give me the fucking phone," Calvin told him sternly. Alan replied while handing it off, "You're no fun. I really don't think she's going to get butt hurt over answering our questions when we're all literally in the same jacked up boat." Holly's voice came over the headpiece, "You're right for once."

"Hello, Doc. I think you know what we're going to ask, so let's cut to the chase for once," Calvin told her bluntly. She replied, "Now is not the time to be thinking about fornicating."

"What?" Calvin asked in confusion and surprise.

"I could ask you the same thing, pervert. I know how one track you can be."

He heard a little giggle in her voice. Calvin looked at the phone wondering if she'd lost her mind. "Oh, lighten up. I just re-killed several of my comrades that turned into zombies. You don't hear me being all cranky. Plus, we're not dead! Plan B totally worked!"

"Worked? Are you serious? Did the plan involve our friends turning into zombies, imbeciles or food for the undead? The one damned time we truly need some fucking guidance, you think it's the perfect moment to be a smartass! If you don't give a shit about getting out of this system alive, tell me now so I can save myself the headache!" He shouted at her, losing all his temper. His frustration and fear dumped out in those words as he gripped the phone. Holly spoke plainly, "Calm down, Petty Officer. I've gotten you and those who are left out of one hole and I will get us out of this one. What I can tell you right now is to get your asses to engineering, but I think you already knew that."

"Way to have trust in me for once. Do you have any real information for us, or are you just going to state the obvious?" he asked her, clinching his teeth. He grasped the phone hard enough to leave fingerprints on the handle. She responded bluntly, "You wanted to make sure there was still a hierarchy on this ship. Well, you just got that confirmation. Keep a cool head or we're really going to be dead. Now get that initiative going. Also send both the brain damaged and undamaged organics to me. I have experiments to run."

"Figures. Roger, out," Calvin hung up the phone and punched the blockhead. "Fucking loon!"

He looked over at his teammates, "Wait here."

"She didn't tell you much, huh?" Valery guessed correctly. "Even in the darkest of hours, she's being vague."

"She's definitely an opportunist. Can't knock her for that," Alan told him with a smile. Calvin smiled back, "I'll knock her for being a cold-hearted witch."

"Take pictures when you do!" he encouraged him. Damon laughed, "No balls! You're just talking out your ass!"

"Want to bet?" Alan asked him, smiling at the idea of attacking her. Damon laughed, "What do you want to wager?"

"Focus!" Calvin shouted at them. The other four

Calvin replicates walked up to him. "She didn't tell you shit. Did she?"

"And bears shit in the woods, space is cold, and there are more airplanes in the sea than subs in the sky! How's the rest of the ship looking?" Calvin Alpha asked them as his eyes twitched in frustration. "Thankfully, the armory is secure. The lockers and main armory have been designated as rally points for all remaining sentient crewmembers and operators," one responded.

"The grunts and zombies dominate the engineering spaces, too many by the sounds of it. They're doing some sick…" he paused, shivering in disgust.

Calvin sighed, "Got the idea. This ship has two main spaces, right?" They nodded, "Here's the plan. Two teams will escort the brain damage, wounded and regulars alike to medical. Another will go and link up with the armory. I'll go with a team to a main space. After everyone secures their areas, start sweeping the ship for zombies and grunts."

"Shouldn't we be worried about the bridge and Command Information Center, too?" one of the leaders queried. Calvin replied, "Then sweep those sections first after we secure the spaces that are vital to us not blowing up prematurely. Are there any other questions?"

"Why would Holly want all the organics in the

infirmary? They could assist with getting the ship back up and operational," another Calvin replicate asked. Calvin replied, "Said something about experimentation, probably nothing good."

"I don't think the grunts would be too cooperative around her. Any ideas there?" a counterpart pointed out as a couple grunts attempted to run away. Calvin came up with this, "Either find a laser pointer for them to chase or put leashes on them."

"We're going to treat them like animals? These are our comrades we're talking about!" one of the crewmen yelled. Just then, a large farting noise came from the direction of the grunts, breaking the mood. Calvin smiled, "We'll worry about their dignity when they get it back. Our focus is staying alive. Anything else?" They rocked their heads from side to side. "Then let's take back our ship!"

CHAPTER 11
SWEEP
DATE UNKNOWN
S.I.S. LEONIDAS
AIRLOCK

"IT'S cramped in here," Damon complained as he felt his way around. Rose cried in shock, "Take your hand off my ass before I cut it off!"

"None of us are touching you, Rose," Beth told her. A hollow laugh echoed through the airlock. Valery sighed, "How did we not see those grunts?"

The brain damaged man and woman looked up and smiled sheepishly as they kept poking at Rose. Alan scoffed, "To think, these were once well-educated officers."

"Bind them up and throw them back into the hanger. The others will take them to the infirmary," Calvin told him, starting to get aggravated. "Also try to pay more attention to your surroundings. If dumb grunts can sneak up on us, so can zombies."

The man and woman were pushed out into the airlock where they were taken away. Rose asked curiously, "Why where they only touching me?"

"Take it as a compliment!" Valery smiled and playfully slapped Rose on the butt.

The door closed again. Damon asked, "Sure we couldn't bring any other types of jury-rigged energy weapons with us? These makeshift crossbows seem shady at best."

"Those were the best things we could come up in the little time we had. Don't like it? You still got your makeshift pike. Use that," Calvin told him bluntly.

"Now let's fucking go already!" Calvin ordered, and Rose forced the door open. Valery and Calvin went out first, throwing flares down the passageway, illuminating the path before them with red lights. As they went forward, Rose closed the door behind them and walked backwards with Alan covering their rear. They came to a four-way intersection. Calvin covered left, and Valery covered right. Both threw flares in each direction checking for anything that moved. A couple of grunts saw the light and screamed. Valery was so shocked she nearly fired her weapon. The grunts ran off into the darkness crying all the while. Damon asked, "Should we go get them?"

"No. Main space is the priority. We'll get them

later," Calvin responded. Damon and Beth went forward and covered the front. Once Rose and Alan passed behind them, they took the center. Calvin and Valery covered the rear. Once they reached the first set of torches, another couple was thrown ahead of them. They landed at the feet of a zombie. She looked at them and let out a high-pitched scream. They heard her footsteps stomping toward them. Alan and Rose pulled metal shields off their backs and clamped them onto their arms. The zombie kept charging. Valery and Calvin fired metal bolts at the zombie, hitting her in the kneecaps. The creature fell to the ground and crawled forward rasping. Rose rushed its head with her shield. They kept moving forward down the passageway as more zombies charged at them. This time Calvin and Valery managed to get head shots on their targets. One of them leaped forward, dodging the bolts. The two of them quickly reloaded as the zombie got right up to them. Two more bolts were fired. This zombie managed to grab both bolts out of midair and jab Rose and Alan in their eyes with them. They cried in pain as they were shoved aside. Valery got grabbed and thrown forward. Calvin quickly swung up with his knife at the monster's head. The zombie caught the knife with both hands and pulled him forward, trying to bite Calvin's right arm. The sharp teeth were making progress as they slowly went through the armor.

Rose swung around and stabbed the zombie in the head. It dropped to the deck. Calvin had the additional horror of seeing his face on one of the zombies. Valery got up, swinging her rifle around rapidly. jabbing the oncoming zombies in the head. The muzzle of the weapons popped the heads of the zombies with a wet crunching sound. Calvin pushed the wounded Rose and Alan towards Valery. She leaped back behind them as the zombies came after her. The two upfront shoved their shields forward pushing the biters back. Damon shouted, "It is just me or are some of these fuckers getting smarter?"

"Maybe they had something or someone good to eat," Calvin said as he moved his bitten arm around. Pain shot through his body. Both Rose and Alan removed the objects that got stuck in their eye sockets, grunting in pain. "The one time we need our fucking face masks, the one time!"

"Like we're ever going to have what we need when we really need it! Get real!" Calvin declared. His wrist and arm felt like they were on fire. Alan laughed, "Get real? We're artificial beings that were programmed to think we're human. Oh, yeah, we also must deal with zombies. So, what's real again?"

"Not getting killed, how about that?" Calvin huffed, still shaking his arm around. Without warning,

Valery cut off his right arm from the elbow down. He let out a scream from the pain and dropped to his knees. He grabbed the bleeding stub as Valery grabbed a torch and cauterized his wound. "What the hell was that for?" Calvin moaned.

She quickly reached down and ripped the armor off the severed arm. The flesh was starting to decay around the artificial bones. She attached the shield to Calvin's stump. He was able to move it around easily. He grabbed a pike with his other arm and took the forward position.

Valery turned to Alan and Rose, "This is going to hurt."

She stuck a flare to their empty eye sockets, cauterizing their wounds. Both let out a cry in the process. Beth asked, "Why are you cauterizing their wounds?"

"Don't want to risk infection. If you haven't noticed, our healing abilities aren't working right now. And if you don't want to turn into one of those things, this is what we must do," she replied.

"Rose, trade places with Damon. Let's keep going!" Calvin ordered as they shuffled around. The team kept moving down the octagon shaped passageway, sticking close together. They managed to work though the excruciating pain they were in. Soon, they came to a red and yellow phone box. As they moved toward it, a grunt came from around the corner screaming, being chased by a zombie. The zombie leaped on the grunt, forcing it to the ground and biting out a chunk of his skull. Blood squirted out as the zombie drank the fluid that oozed out. The victim's eyes rolled to the back of his head. The body went limp and dropped to the deck, dead. The zombie let out a long sigh and looked over at them, ready for her next meal. She pulled out two axes and juggled them around while licking her teeth. Calvin snapped, "Shoot her!"

Alan and Beth fired their crossbows. She managed to throw her axes forward, grab the bolts and throw them back. One bolt hit Calvin's shield and the other went into Beth's stomach. She let out a cry and fell backward. Both axes hit the wall and fell to the ground, a loud clang echoing in the passageway. The zombie leaped over Calvin and Valery as they both tried to catch her on the overhead with their shields. She was able to reach the axes and swiped up at Valery, catching her in the neck. Valery tried to move out of the way but got her throat cut. She dropped backwards, holding her neck. Damon turned around and stabbed the zombie through the chest, pinning her to the deck. She managed to bite through his armor and take a chunk out of his foot. He screamed as he dropped his shield on her head and smashed it. Rose quickly cut off his leg from the knee down and cauterized it. He yelled in pain as he was burned. Calvin did his best to cauterize Valery's wound. She let out a couple of tears but didn't make any noise. Alan carried Beth in his arms as she pushed the rod out of her stomach and stabbed herself with a torch to burn the wound. She gritted her teeth and moaned loudly in the process. Damon managed to hobble along on his single leg, using the wall for leverage. When they reached the phone, they team leaned against the bulkhead trying to compose itself. Calvin reached forward and grabbed the phone. Damon dialed the number for him. "Team one; reporting in," Calvin announced.

Soon others responded, "Team three, medical. Copy."

"Team four, main armory. Copy."

"Team five, back up armory. Copy."

"Team two?" Calvin asked. No one responded. "Team two?" Still no response. "Got to assume team two is KIA. Shit!"

Holly's voice came on, "Team one, what is your status?"

He looked at his hurting friends, "We're combat ineffective. All of us are jacked up in one way or another. We underestimated these zombies to say the least."

"The more they feed, the stronger they get. After they took out a couple of operators they found out that the organics are just as good to feed off as the augmented…and easier," she told them. Calvin replied, "Easier? They got us pretty good."

"Guess you ran into your share of them. Another team will deal with the engineering space. The rest of you get to medical. Just a warning, you're going to run into the remains of team two."

"Thanks for being straightforward for once. Team one out," Calvin slammed the phone back into its holder and gasped in pain, "We're going to medical. Brace yourselves for more hard asses."

"Are you kidding me?" asked Alan. Calvin took his place next to Valery as she held her shields up. Damon was about to raise his crossbow, but Calvin stopped him. "Attach this first," he said, handing him an explosive.

"I thought we weren't trying to cause damage," Damon said while he and Rose attached the explosives to the bolts. "The explosive yield isn't that high. Besides, now isn't the time to worry about collateral damage," Calvin responded.

The six of them turned the opposite way from the engineering space and headed toward medical. They threw flares forward to illuminate their path. Save the noise from their shuffling feet and the hiss of the flares, the hall was quiet. That didn't last long. As they moved closer to the medical area, the sound of breaking bones and sloshing blood got louder. It sounded disgustingly sloppy as the zombies chewed with their mouths open. This time, the team threw fragmental grenades instead of flares. In a brief flash of light, Calvin's team saw the zombies happily consuming people who used to be their friends, blue and red blood dripping on the deck floor. The zombies let out a quick scream before they exploded. Most of them vanished in the explosion that followed.

Calvin's team threw flares forward. There was nothing left in front of them but a cloud of smoke. They stood there for what felt like an hour, waiting for something to move. Slowly, the shadows of six more zombies appeared ahead of them. When they noticed Calvin's team, they charged. Damon and Rose fired their explosive bolts, taking out three of them. The zombies were shredded to bits by the force of the explosion and shrapnel that followed. The remaining three snuck right up to them in the confusion. One zombie ripped the shield from Calvin's stump and jabbed at him with sharp fingers. Calvin managed to dodge his attacker. From behind, two more zombies showed up and started attacking Alan and Beth. Alan let out a loud scream as his other eye was poked out. He franticly used his shield as a club and started smashing in the direction of the zombie. Beth got into a wrestling match as the zombie tried to steal her shield. They both slammed against the bulkhead while fighting for control of the metal board. Rose went down on the ground holding her face as her second eye was lost, too. Damon slammed the zombie against the bulkhead and crushed its skull, brains splattering across the deck. He went over to help Valery who kept her zombie pinned against the bulkhead as well. It managed to break free. Valery quickly cut the legs out from under it but not before it got a bite out of Damon's good leg. He screamed in fury as he had to cut off his other leg from the knee down. Calvin stabbed the Zombie up through the jaw, killing it. After letting it drop, he stabbed the zombie Beth was battling with in the head.

Suddenly, several flares got thrown their way. To Calvin's relief, he saw other operators coming toward them. He lifted his good hand up when a zombie leaped from the shadows and bit it. He screamed loudly as Valery smashed the zombie's head in with her shield and cut off Calvin's infected hand. He dropped to the deck screaming in pain. With no more zombies in sight, the operators helped Calvin's team to the medical bay. Alan and Rose had to be guided down the passageway while Beth and Damon were carried. Calvin walked. The team ran past several re-dead zombies, mutilated organics and operators, but they were too busy to notice them. They reached the infirmary where another team was standing guard. Piles of re-dead zombies were in front of them, serving as makeshift barricades. The infirmary was in chaos. There were several operators and crewmen. All were wounded. The nurses and doctors worked with what they had to patch everyone. Holly came up to them and started to sedate each one of them. Calvin looked at her with dismay as he kept his stubs under his armpits. She gasped when she saw them, "Wow. You really got chewed up out there."

Calvin replied sarcastically, "You don't say," and stuck his tongue out at her. She stabbed it with a needle and injected him with a sedative. "Sorry about this," Holly expressed, "but it's easier to work on you when you're sleep."

Calvin aimed his stubs at his crotch and whispered, "Work on..." but before he could finish his thought, Calvin was down on the deck, out cold.

Chapter 12
Clear
Date Unknown
Leonidas
Infirmary

CALVIN opened his eyes after an unrestful slumber. His eyes seemed to be able to adjust to the light on their own. The infirmary was illuminated by several emergency lights that came on from overhead. There were cans filled with red and blue bandages nearby. Calvin gasped as he instinctively reached up to his head. Two bone looking limbs came up at him. His new hands looked like just they were just bone and ligaments. Skin slowly moved over the exposed artificial muscle.

He looked around. The others sat around quietly. Calvin could hear banging sounds from the mess decks next to the medical bay. Grunts screamed and threw themselves against the walls, trying to escape. It sounded like there were hundreds of them. He saw Alan and Rose. Both looked like they had dim light bulbs in their eye sockets. Damon had two new legs, Beth had a T-shaped scar on her stomach, and Valery had a scar across her throat.

Now that they were in the light, he finally got a good look at Damon and Beth. Damon had a bald head, dark skin, rounded gold eyes and a scar down his face. Beth had red hair, brown eyes and a pale complexion. Valery came up to Calvin and asked in an artificial voice, "How are you holding up, Cal?"

"For being lunchmeat, I'm okay, Val. Where's Holly?" Calvin wondered as he watched his left hand heal on its own. The artificial flesh moved up the metal bones fast. His thumb was already looking normal. Holly walked out of one of the mess decks covered in dirt and wiping herself off with a rag, rage showing on her face. Calvin bit the inside of his cheek, straining not to laugh at the sight. Holly went to the sink and rapidly splashed water on herself to get clean. He could barely hear her grumbling to herself, "Dumbasses!"

"Holly. I got to ask…" he said as she turned around with fury in her eyes. She composed herself as she finished cleaning off her face, "I shouldn't even be mad. We're alive, and we can get out of the current situation we're in. But I'm really tired of dealing with poo flinging morons!"

"Holly, tell us what in the hell is going on," Calvin

asked pointedly. She started pulling off her scrubs and yelled, "You want to know what's going on? My own comrades just threw their bodily fluids on me! They went from professionals to the equivalent of animals! I'm having a really bad day right now despite the miracle!"

"Miracle my ass. What the hell is going on?" Calvin snapped. She smiled bitterly as she lifted a finger up in the air. Holly pulled a flask from her pocket and took a swig, "You want everything? Here goes. After we all got sent off to die, I started working on a plan to save our asses. I found a third-party contact who said she could help. Said contact encouraged her faction to act, which would work out in our favor. Apparently, she wanted to damage the Claw Empire, and this gave her organization the perfect opportunity to do that. That act helped change the Claw's mind about using us as scapegoats. However, there were some miscalculations with the prototype weapons. They worked just fine back in the Sol system, but they didn't work the same here. Different stars, different effects. The bomb was supposed to use the sun to send an energy pulse set to mentally castrate anyone who was awake in the system. Unfortunately, with this star, it caused a zombie apocalypse to occur. Thankfully, I treated the pulse like an EMP. I was able to force a shutdown and knocked out most of the pulse signals before they affected the whole system. Like I said, it only works on active minds."

Calvin scoffed angrily, "You really thought it was a good idea to make a deal with *a third party*, some random ass person you just met? Wait a second; you used this weapon in the home system? What the hell is wrong with you?"

"What's wrong with me? I'm just trying to save our asses, yours included! Why worry about the assholes back in the Sol system anyway? Do I have to remind you that the Spartans screwed us, used us, and sent us off die? As for the Claw, they were a few seconds away from turning you all into Swiss cheese. I'm not losing any sleep over any pain I have inflicted on them." Holly shouted, trying to reassure him that her actions were just.

"If we survive this, we're going to have words," Damon said pointedly. Holly replied, "Cry all you want about your hurt morality. You're able to do it because of my actions! Don't ever forget that."

"All right. Moving on for the moment, tell us about this contact of yours. I mean didn't you find it strange that she was so willing to cut a deal with you? Why the hell would she do that?" Valery asked her, straining her voice box.

Holly smiled, "Let's just say I have an ace in the hole they want. Leave it at that for now. Frist things last again, we need to secure the rest of the ship. We have teams clearing out the engineering spaces as we speak. The remaining organics are doing what repairs they can. I've also managed to repair some of your weapons, so you can fire projectiles again. You're welcome for everything by the way." She grabbed a box and opened it. In it were six pulse pistols. "Might not be as powerful as plasma rounds, but at least they'll get the job done. I also had your armored suits repaired. Now when those fuckers bite, they'll get a shock."

The nurses brought in their armor and placed it next to each of them. All the suits looked hastily put together with weld marks still fresh. The team shrugged as each member quickly donned a protective suit. Holly went on, "I need you all to get to the main bridge as soon as possible. It's not going to be easy though." She brought up surveillance footage of zombies wondering around, "As you can see, there are several zombies between you and the bridge, and they're hungry."

"Yeah, thanks for the information!" Calvin grumbled as he put on his helmet. Rose asked, "You patched us up. What about the zombies and grunts? Can you fix them, too?"

"Zombies...no. Grunts... maybe, but one thing at a time. Focus on the immediate peril first," she responded as the doors opened with more wounded coming in. All of them were missing limbs, their armored suits scratched and dented in. "Get going!"

The six of them left the infirmary. In the passageway were several other operatives and crewmembers leaning against the bulkheads recovering from their wounds. A couple more grunts were being forced into the mess decks. They passed by the doors and saw through the round window all of them trying to get out. The guards kept them under control by using a laser pointer. They aimed it up at the ceiling, and the grunts followed the beam. Rose exclaimed in dismay, "They're acting like house pets."

"We'll worry about them later, Rose," Calvin told her, focusing on the task at hand. He was furious that Holly would pull such a stunt. Yeah, she said it was to save them, but at what cost? He shivered as he thought of the home system and what became of it. The others followed him through a set of doors and closed them after they passed by. They saw signs of fighting with blue and red stains on the bulkhead. There were clusters of flesh, organs and bones on the deck as well. Beth spoke up, "This suck, but I'm not even mad. At least we're not dead."

Calvin looked back at her, "Are you kidding me?"

"No. Why be mad? We got even with the fuckers that threw us to the wolves," she responded.

Valery chimed in, "Am I the only one wondering how Holly managed to fool the Spartans *and* the Claw?"

Damon shrugged, "Probably because no one pays attention to the walking dead until it's too late."

"Speaking of the dead, let's focus on making sure the zombies stay that way," Calvin interjected with renewed vigor. As they moved along the passageway, Beth asked, "Do you think it would be wrong to fool around with the grunts?"

Everyone stopped and looked back at her, "What?!"

She explained, "Come on. It might snap them back to their old selves, kind of like how Calvin got his first augmentation from sleeping with that android prostitute."

"How did you know that?" Calvin asked as everyone looked at him strangely. "So, what was Kathryn like?" Valery wondered out loud. Calvin looked back at her and smiled, "Wouldn't you know already?"

"At least I remember! Your memory is still shit," she quickly tried to change the subject. He smirked knowing she got augmented the same way he did.

"Didn't someone say something about priorities and focus?" Rose piped in. Calvin grumbled again at being outwitted. "You got me there. Let's keep moving."

They kept going through the passageway, seeing

more death as they went along. Valery asked, "Think Yeager and Kathryn are still alive?"

He stopped in his tracks with those names hitting him like a lightning bolt. Quickly, he pushed the thoughts aside and replied, "Knowing them, they'd find a way to persevere. We'll find a way back to them. Okay?"

"Don't you mean *if* we get out of here?" Beth asked him. He told her, "We'll get out of here. Besides, you all are more family than they'll ever be."

"Well, isn't that touching?" Alan said, patting him on the back, "But don't get sappy on me. We got things to re-kill."

"Sounds like a good time to me," Damon said when suddenly the ship rocked violently and all of them went up into the overhead.

Chapter 13
Date Unknown
Landing
S.I.S. Leonidas
Passageway

CALVIN got up and pushed the door open in front of him with a loud slam. Everyone ran into the passageway, using their boosters to stop themselves from hitting the overhead as they floated through the air. Calvin rocketed forward, following the others, "Gun it to the bridge!"

"Way ahead of you!" Valery shouted as she stabbed the zombie straggler in front of her. Rose and Alan went past her and shot five zombies right in the head in rapid succession. They went flying backward from the impact, their heads cracking against the bulkhead. Their limp bodies bounced around the passageway as the ship spun around. Beth and Damon ripped open the doors to an elevator shaft, "Down we go!"

Calvin quipped, "Just not all the way."

"You never go all the way," Alan joked as Calvin replied, "Oh, I've got proof I have."

Valery snapped at them, "Just go!"

The six members of the squad flew down to the command deck near the center of the ship. The doors opened to zombies, at least a dozen of them. They all screamed when they saw the operators, eager to feed. The living rocketed back up the shaft in a panic as arms reached for them. The zombies followed, leaping from side to side to get closer to the operatives. The team fired, hitting several zombies in the head. They splattered against the overhead. One zombie managed to grab Valery. "Not this time!" she shouted. Valery boosted up as the zombie tried to bite her. She turned around, cut off the top of its head and kicked it away. Alan threw a grenade down into the doorway. It went right back up to the overhead and exploded. Several body parts flew past them along with metal fragments. The six of them flew through the ruptured door and onto the command deck. The path was clear, and the six of them reached the last set of doors that led to the spherical bridge.

Beth and Damon pulled the doors open, and the others charged in. Inside, one zombie floated in the center of the room. He had Calvin's face and smiled at the sight of them entering. There were several dead bodies floating around the zombie with their brains ripped from their skulls. Damon chuckled, "I got this."

He started to throw a grenade at the Calvin zombie. The zombie licked a knife and threw it straight for Damon, hitting him in the hand. The grenade flew. "Damn!" he yelled as Beth quickly cut off his infected hand. The explosive went off, knocking Beth and Damon into the bulkhead and out cold. The zombie ran up to them and grabbed pistols from their armor while dodging shots from their four teammates. It managed to dodge every round before firing back. Rose and Alan flew backward into the bulkhead, bleeding from multiple wounds. Calvin remembered their abilities and shouted, "Deus ex Machina!"

Calvin and Valery boosted forward at the zombie, firing away. They managed to knock one of the pistols out of the undead's hands. He leaped over at them pulling out another knife. The zombie swung it at Calvin while Calvin swung right back. The blades bounced off each other as they collided. The zombie fired blindly at Valery with its remaining pistol and kept Calvin at bay by jabbing at him with its long nails. One jab knocked Calvin's pistol away.

The zombie then turned to Beth, who was waking back up. The zombie tried to shoot her, but Calvin managed to kick it hard enough to cause the shot to miss.

Valery got three hits in on the zombie's torso. Shards of its armor and flesh vaporized into the air. Calvin then cut off one of its hands and stabbed the zombie in the head. It dropped to the floor, no longer a threat. "Clear!" Calvin yelled.

"Are you going to shout Deus ex Machina every time we use our enhanced abilities?" Valery asked Calvin as he went over to help Alan and Rose. "It does sound cool. Doesn't it?" he replied.

"The first time, kind of. Now it's a little corny," Alan told him bluntly. "We're not superheroes, just lucky."

Beth spoke, "Hate to interrupt, but I got the controls back online." Lights flashed on and images streamed across the screen. The surface of the planet below was getting closer and closer. Calvin and Valery boosted toward the control panel, quickly punching the holographic buttons that were supposed to move the ship back up and out of harm's way. As the rest of the team made its way to the deck, Calvin held his position in front of the control panel. He activated the ship's thrusters to start slowing the vessel down. They were skimming across an ocean, a city popping up over the horizon. "Up!" Beth yelled in panic. Calvin shouted, "What do you think I'm trying to do over here?"

"Shit! We can barely go up! The engines are still

jacked!" Valery realized. Calvin sighed, "Then I guess we'll have to play a little game of dodge the skyscrapers."

"This ship is fucking huge! How the hell are you going to fly this thing through the city?" she asked. Damon rose up to the weapons control console, "With explosives!"

He fired a blue colored torpedo at the cylinder-shaped buildings, sending a shockwave that shattered the glass off them. They fell like dominos but not fast enough. "Going vertical!"

"What?" Everyone asked as the vessel tilted up, the engines struggling. Its triangular edge scraped the road as the ship entered the city, pushing away everything not tied down to the side. The thrusters were working overtime to keep the ship from slamming into the surface. The Leonidas just managed to clear the city. Everyone shouted at once, "Mountain!"

"I know!" Calvin yelled as he got the ship level again. He pointed the ship to the sky trying to climb as high as possible, "Come on!"

The mountain got closer and closer. Soon it was all they could see. The ship wasn't going up fast enough, and its sensors could tell. Bells and alarms sounded off, warning them of the potential impact. Calvin sighed, "Brace for shock."

They boosted to the front of the bridge as the top

of the mountain appeared. A violent thud echoed through the ship. Calvin flew forward into the screen ahead of him, caught himself and floated back down to the floor. The others landed next to him. He laughed as the ship stopped moving, "Happy landing…"

CHAPTER 14
BREAK
DATE UNKNOWN
EAGLE'S STABLE
S.I.S. LEONIDAS
BRIDGE

CALVIN opened his eyes. His head felt numb. He gasped as he saw the re-dead zombie under him. Its face was still intact and looked up at him with glazed over eyes. It was like looking into a disgusting mirror seeing the worst version of himself. The skin looked rotted and burned. The zombie still had bits of meat in its teeth. Valery tapped him on his shoulder making him jump, "Calm down! We re-killed all the zombies. You're not dead. Right?"

"I guess," he told her as he moved his limbs around. Already, the crewmen were hard at work fixing what was broken. The images on the round screen became clear again. It was a sunny day on top of the grassy mountain. Umbrella shaped trees were scattered about, and the mountain's tall peak looked over a city in ruins. Images of the Leonidas's Tri-Star shaped hull popped up on the screen showing she had literally moved the top of the mountain upon impact. The ground where the ship landed was rounded from the energy shields that cushioned the impact of the crash. Alan cheered, "We made it!"

"Hate to say it, but we're not out of the woods yet. There's still more we need to take care of," Valery motioned for him to follow her. They both joined the others at the doorway. The six of them had to use their boosters to travel up the elevator shaft, back to the infirmary. All of them relaxed their armored suits as they felt air go against their bodies. Beth commented while looking up at the cracked overhead, "That was one hell of a fight and one hell of a flight."

"It's not every day we get to kill zombie versions of ourselves. Is it?" Calvin said as he passed by a re-dead zombie that looked like him on the deck. The body's head was split in two with the brains and blood leaking out. He gasped with shivers going up his spine. Valery pleaded with him quietly as she could, "It's okay now. Please stay the fuck together, because I'm just a few steps away from freaking out myself."

"Guess we're still human... sort of." He smiled at her. Alan told them, "Doc is waiting."

"Shit," they both grumbled as they got to the infirmary. Holly walked out, her green coveralls covered in blue and red blood. She was laughing to herself, "We did it! We're alive!"

She got handed a piece of metal with writing etched into it. Mumbling to herself she sighed, "I really miss my holo pad."

"Miss your holo pad? That's terrible! How will you survive?" Alan asked her sarcastically. She looked up at him glaring for a few second before composing herself. "Really? You won't be here without me. Mind your manners."

"Seeing as how we're not in peril right now, we need to clear some things up, like you being a fucking murderer!" Calvin's pent up rage bubbling to the surface. Valery grabbed his shoulder, "You're not helping things."

Holly smiled and scoffed, "You think you got any moral ground to stand on? We're all murderers on this ship. None of you are in any position to judge me when your hands are just as dirty as mine. What is there to clear up anyway? Yes, we landed the ship, but it's not like we're safe. We're stuck on a planet that has several billion cyber zombies on it, and they all think we're on the menu. I'm working on a solution rather than being a cry baby."

"Now when you say solution…," Rose asked her

hesitantly. Holly gave them a long look resisting the urge to roll her eyes, "I got us out of one hole. I can get us out of this one."

"Your back up plan is working out so," Valery let out a sarcastic scoff. Her eyes went wide as she thought out loud, "Wait a second. Who's in charge? I thought medical personnel couldn't take command of a ship."

Holly laughed as she tapped the metal plank, "As the only surviving officer of this ship... actually of what's left of the fleet. I assumed positional authority. Wait, there's one more thing that I did. What was it?" She paused sarcastically thinking to herself before going, "Oh yeah! I'm the one that saved your asses, proving I'm capable!"

"For the sake of argument, what is your plan to fly off this rock?" Damon asked her in a tired voice.

Holly smiled as she set the metal pad down. When she looked back up she told them, "You're all not going to like what I have in mind. Yet, how badly do you all not want to be zombie meat? Willing to do anything?"

"Anything could be a lot of things. Would you please stop being coy and tell us what screwed up shit you want us to do this time!" Valery snapped at her losing her patience. Holly scowled at her and as she kept from losing her own temper she told them, "I want you to assist with the augmentation of the organic crewmembers of this ship."

"What?" All six of them said at once looking at her in confusion. Beth started laughing, "How are we going to do that? Magic?"

"No. STI. One of my many contingencies." Holly told them as Rose added it up in her head, "You want us to screw the grunts? They can't consent! Not to mention STI? We're not organic! We can't have one of those… right?"

Holly smiled broadly, "You can. You're all made with the equipment for a reason, not just making more fodder for the cannons to shoot at. It's how you all got upgraded in the first place. The injection I gave you should make you all far more contagious. No one has the antidote or protection here, one of the reasons why none of you were able to infect anyone else back in the home system." She told them while juggling a syringe.

"Wait; couldn't we just use that memory juice stuff to make them remember?" Beth recommended as Rose joined in, "Why the hell not some kind of transplant?"

Damon added, "Wait, what does fornicating with the grunts have anything to do with us fly off back into space? Couldn't you just take samples from us and give it to them?"

Holly went over to her equipment and snapped, "See all of this. It doesn't work. We can't come back from the dead anymore. We can't replicate anyone else. I thought about every alternative!" She snapped at them losing her cool. She calmed herself and went on, "Might be a cold hearted witch, but I'm also quite thorough. Am I getting through to you all on how broken our shit is? Most of the equipment is fucked up beyond recognition. I know I use the word miracle a lot, but it is a miracle that we aren't zombies or flat as a pancake. The most surefire way to infect them is to go through the genitals interacting. Why the hell are you all being so hesitant? The others seemed to be okay with doing what's necessary. Hell, most of the regular organic crewmen volunteered to get altered. I think the grunts would do the same if they could. It's implied consent seeing how it's the only way to reverse the lobotomy jobs done to their heads! Hell, there's nothing left in their heads but primal impulses! Again, am I getting through to you all?"

"I really don't think that makes screwing the mentally impaired just to improve them, is okay. I also don't think that any consent is implied. What the hell is wrong with you anyway?" Valery told her freaked out that she had to explain why she wasn't interested.

"For crying out loud, they are mentally castrated!

151

You'll be filling in a blank space and giving them what they lost back. Hell, you'll be giving them combat knowledge too, so they'll be able to fight as well as increasing our odds of survival. If you're lobotomized, wouldn't you want a fix? Needs of the many outweigh your damned comfort zones! I mean how is being turned into zombie meat not motivation enough to screw for life? What is wrong with you people? How many times do I need to mention priorities?" Holly shouted at them in frustration. Again, she had to recompose herself.

"It's your fault that we're in this mess in the first place. I mean is there a limit with you? Committing mass genocide to save our asses wasn't enough? You really want us to force ourselves on others?" Calvin tried to reason with her. She laughed, "We've been getting figuratively forced on for long enough. Your hesitation is killing me and everyone on this ship. My actions saved us, and we will get power too. Got to point out that the crewmembers aren't going to be able to get the repairs done fast enough before the hordes of zombies show up. We don't have enough operators to fend them off either. We're going to need more functional people. Augmented people are easier and faster to reproduce than normal ones. Not to mention augmented personal work better in space than organic ones do. Want more? Think long term, blood bath is just getting started. We're in for a long violent fucking war ahead of us. Not only dealing with the zombies but killing anyone else who stands in our way. Now please use your equipment that you're given! Most would kill to have a set of two and four!"

"Wait... two? You guys have more than one and two?" Beth asked with curiosity. Alan laughed nervously, "So it's not normal to be a two by four?"

"You wouldn't have believed us if we told you. It's not a priority to flash them in the middle of fighting," Damon said. Calvin laughed, "Guess there were positives to being created by perverts. Still, some things are too much. We're not going to use the imperiled as playthings. End of story."

"Fuck it! Fine. I'll allow you all to take a load off in the berthing. There's something special for you there if you want to take it. It'll make you feel good for a minute," she told them as they looked at each other skeptically, "Really?"

"Yes. Like I said, others will do what needs to be done. Go before I change my mind," she told them as they promptly left the infirmary. Damon spoke up, "This feels too good to be true."

"Shut up. Let's take the break while we can," Valery told him as she removed more of her armor. The others followed suit as they slowly walked to the berthing. They went down the ladder well to the doors. Alan laughed, "You all don't have to pay for it for once!"

They entered the berthing, dark except for small red lights. In front of them was a bowl of pills. Alan laughed, "Sweet, drugs!"

"Sure that's a good idea?" Calvin asked as Alan took a handful. "Like things could get any worse?" Alan replied as he downed the drugs.

Everyone shrugged as they impulsively went for the pills and quickly gulped them down. One by one they started falling on the ground. Valery sighed, "I think we made a mistake."

"Only one of many," Calvin told her as he went face first into the wooden deck. He heard boot steps coming towards them. Calvin managed to roll over in time to see a heel come down on his head.

CHAPTER 15
DREAM
DATE UNKNOWN
S.I.S. LEONIDAS
BERTHING

CALVIN opened his eyes. Everything seemed off. He was in the berthing on the wooden floor, laying between the racks. The red lights disoriented him as he felt around. His hands landed on something soft and smooth. It...no she, was underneath him. Calvin let out a gasp, shooting up quickly. He looked down at the woman with shock running though his body, "Oh shit! It wasn't my fault! I didn't have a choice!"

She was still, with only the slightest movement to show she was breathing. With one hand he reached down and pushed her hair to the side. He suddenly heard Jane's voice, "Was it good for you?"

He quickly moved back seeing Jane smiling up at him with her red hair and wide smile, "You've always been so lucky."

"This can't be real," he told her as he backed off.

"This isn't numb nuts. You're dreaming. Is this life everything you thought it would be?" The Doctor asked as he held a martini up while sitting in front of a wooden table with holographic images being projected behind him. With a closer look, he saw himself, a woman on top of him moaning as she went up and down. "Wait a second! No! Make it stop!"

"Did you really thing it was a good idea to take drugs that were just laying around?" the Doc told him, and Calvin snapped back, "Fuck you, mental projection! You know I wanted to get jacked up!"

"There's a price for everything old man!" his son Yeager told him mockingly. Calvin rolled his eyes, "Okay, I'm ready to wake up now!"

A replicate of Calvin walked by him, "Why leave when the fun has just begun?"

"What fun?" He asked as the Calvin replicate dropped down on top of Jane and stroked her hair, "Despite being doped up and being taken advantage of by a lobotomized lady, you're having fun with that woman, aren't you?"

"What?"

Alec Dumont yelled at him, "A sick bastard like you would enjoy something like that. Be the Alpha right?

156

No matter who it hurts!"

"Why feel bad about it. Everything we feel is just programmed in anyway. Everything you feel is just electrical impulse that most would call fake. What can we expect from an artificial being?" Calvin's replicate told him as he gave Jane a kiss. She shouted, "You couldn't really care for anyone. You have no concept of love."

"I cannot be this self-loathing! I think all of you know that the real-life Jane led me on! Who are you to lecture me about love?" Calvin shouted at him as Jane laughed, "We're in your head! We can lecture you all we want, silly."

"You're the one who pictured someone you thought loved you while you ravaged that poor impaired woman to cope with being a slave! Whatever makes you feel like a good monster; right?" Alec laughed. The Calvin replicate looked back with a smirk, "We are good monsters. Aren't we? Just following orders."

He thrust his hips towards Jane as she gasped loudly, "We only obey like slaves. Keep telling yourself you're fighting for freedom."

"Oh fuck you all! You're part of me! Don't judge!" Calvin shouted enraged. Yeager laughed, "Everyone gets judged here, bastard!"

"Why would anyone like a monster like you?" Jane

asked him in between moans.

"You were sent out on a suicide mission to be disposed after all. You only got saved by an even sicker woman who has no morals," the Doctor told him while juggling a pistol in his hands. A woman suddenly appeared in front of him. She looked like Holly, except blue eyes instead of gold. She had on an old combat uniform. Calvin could see the name Murthy on her chest. He recognized her as the Doctor he saw when he thought he shifted through time. She smiled, "You were an excellent weapon after all. You served my counterpart well."

As his double kept moving his body on top of Jane's, he looked up at Calvin, "You didn't feel bad about all that collateral damage with the civilians. People were just going about their lives until you charged in guns blazing. Imagine how many billions got crushed, and now are choking to death on the ashes. Not to mention all the poor bastards on this world who are now zombies thanks to you. Your own son is up shit creek to save your sorry ass! Why feel bad about anything?"

"Oh, fuck you again! All of that was out of my control! I'm sick of everyone blaming me for everything. I'm not always wrong!" Calvin shouted at them.

"When are you ever right?" Jane shouted at him. Calvin backed away, "I want to wake up now!"

"You're always trying to shrug off responsibility. Just because 'you're programmed to be a puppet' doesn't make you any less guilty," Yeager shouted at him. Alec laughed, "I'm sure they'll forgive you. You had no control; remember? But does anyone really forgive the tool that committed the crime?"

"Monsters deserve no forgiveness or pity!" Jane shouted at him. Calvin turned around seeing Kathryn standing in front of him, "Doesn't feel good does it?"

"What, the dream? Or having everything come back to haunt me?" he replied, growing frustrated. She stroked his cheek, "To be a victim of your own programming; all your thoughts, hopes, aspirations, even dreams not counting for anything because it's all fake. You're a machine bound to do as it's programmed to. You have no real value at all."

"Fuck you! I'm human!" He shouted at loudly. She reached down and grabbed one of his fingers and ripped off it his hand. He gasped as she showed off his finger with blue blood and wire sticking out of it, "Not anymore! Humans don't bleed blue blood!"

Calvin punched Kathryn in the face, "Fuck you! I didn't ask for you to sleep with me!" He punched her again, "I didn't ask to be a part of this!" Another punch, "I didn't ask to be a father!" Punch, "You made me betray my nation!" Punch! "You used me!" Punch! "You took everything from me!" Punch, "And I'm not a bastard!"

He punched her again as sparks flew out of her head. Yeager grabbed his arm and broke it with a twist of his wrist. Through the loud popping of bones Yeager told him, "You wanted this! All that time talking shit about how cool it would be to operate! So bored with your mundane life as a glorified bureaucrat! An administrator for crying out loud! This is everything you could ever hope for! You're a badass now! Why worry about lost memories when you're even more pathetic now than before?"

Calvin looked back at Alec as he was on top of Jane now with the slapping noise between them getting louder, "You like killing. You love fornicating! You can finally be the badass you always pretended to be no matter who it hurts!"

"Fuck you all! I'm not an asshole!" He shouted. Yeager laughed, "Please, you abandoned your children to suffer an apocalypse, kill whoever you're told to without question, and even force yourself on others. Sounds like being a bastard to me."

Alec leaned down licking the tears off Jane's face, "You loved this! Still thinking you can help anyone?"

Jane looked up at Calvin as she tried backing away again. "Did you really think our nights together produced nothing?"

"What? You got pregnant too? How would I know that?" Calvin asked in shock. Yeager twisted Calvin's arm in a more painful position, "Made another poor soul to suffer because of your mistakes; didn't you?"

"Let go!" Calvin head butted Yeager and punched him in the head, knocking him down. Suddenly a woman looked up at him. "Why did you leave, Daddy? Why?"

The Doctor laughed, "For the mission!"

"What the fuck is wrong with your mind?" Alec asked him. "Wait, the question should be what's right?" Alec laughed at him.

Calvin closed his eyes and started screaming at the top of his lungs. The woman named Murthy came over to him and touched his shoulders. Yeager backed off. "Don't be a wuss. This is just a dream," she reassured him. Calvin asked, "Who are you?'

"You can think of me as your conviction not to quit. Never say die after all." She told him while grabbing his hands. "Embrace what you are. Don't fight your nature, even if it is artificial."

"Wait a second. I think I know you…" Calvin said as he looked at her closer. He was suddenly on Mars on a clear and sunny day. The two of them were standing in front of a statue of the woman standing over a giant bug's head while crushing it with her boot. In one hand she had a flag staff waving the colors of the Alliance, and in the other hand she had a rifle. He looked down at the inscription, "Helena 'Iron Bitch' Murthy. "Why would I see a dead war hero?" he wondered aloud.

"I created Holly and the Doctor in a manner of speaking. Find me, and there will be a chance for the new humanity that is forming the rise. Don't let this world be your tomb. Don't think about the people you've killed."

"You told me I could time travel? What was that all about? Were you just bullshitting me?" Calvin asked her as she smiled, "All in due time. A chance will come. You can still change things for the better. Don't give up. There are people counting on you all."

The woman claiming to be his daughter appeared as a massive flash of light started destroying the city. She reached for him. As the dust and rubble flew at them, she let out a yell that he heard through the destruction, "Save us!"

CHAPTER 16
FLY
EAGLE STABLE
LEONIDAS
BERTHING

"WAS it good for you, too?" the woman asked Calvin. He scrambled to stand up when he noticed he was still naked. His eyes went wide when he recognized the woman as being the one he converted. She bore a striking resemblance to Jane with her red hair and pale skin. The lady now had on an armored combat suit and looked like she had been in a fight. "Oh, call me Lane."

He looked at her, unsure of what to say or how to act. The feeling of shame and helplessness hit him like a pile of bricks as he remembered what he probably did while drugged. Yet again, he couldn't help but wonder how it happened with her being impaired and him being doped up. Lane smiled at him with a lack of sincerity, "Relax. Just here to fetch you all. Had your rest, time to get back in the fight."

"Still fighting?" Calvin asked as he realized that the zombies must have made it up the mountain. His guilt was replaced by dread knowing what was coming for them. The other five were getting dressed out in their armored suits as quickly as they could put them on. None of them seemed talkative. Lane handed Calvin his armor and green coveralls, "No rest for the wicked, love."

"Rest? What is that? I don't think nightmares count," Calvin said dreading going back up against the zombies again. Lane laughed, "When you can cry a river, I'll give you a damn."

"Guess that's life." Calvin replied to her as he quickly got his coveralls on. Alan shouted, "Can we please not talk right now! I just want to act like I'm in control for once and have guilt-free violence that doesn't hurt anyone!"

"You assisted in the death of billions already. Why start worrying about guilt now?" Lane accused him with a sharp coldness in her voice. The ship rocked from a blast from outside. Lane gestured for them to follow her. Calvin got back into his armored suit quickly. It was like a second skin to him at this point. He caught up with the others as they left the berthing. The ship rocked again as they passed through the damaged passageway. Rose asked, "Danger close?"

"Very. Those bastards are good climbers," Lane told them. It didn't take them long before they were back in the hanger bay where they could hear weapons fire from outside. The doors were open showing the clear sky outside with plumes of smoke rising in the distance. All of them got handed firearms. Rose checked hers and laughed, "Our guns are working again!"

At the doors were makeshift machine gun nests firing away as fast as they could spit out rounds. The barrels were starting to glow red from the heat. Through the weapons fire a voice could be heard shouting, "First rank; fire!"

There was a loud chorus of rifle fire that sounded off all at once. It went silent. The machine guns kept firing as the voice boomed again, "Second rank; fire!"

As the rifles popped off, the seven of them got to the edge of the hanger seeing three lines of operatives near the ship. They were holding back the seemingly endless horde of zombies. The massive horde was tripping over the thousands of slain piling up in front of them. All the zombies had gaping bullet holes in their heads. The slow walkers made them easy pickings for the riflemen picking them off. Whole clusters of the zombies would suddenly have their heads explode in a flash and topple over. The horde kept climbing up the mountain as fast as they could move their decayed bodies. The Claws now had a disgusting gray color skin with wounds that oozed out green liquid. Their four red eyes were now orange. Their arms seemed to be nothing more than five long sets of sharp nails that started from their elbows. They moved on the balls of their deformed feet. They still had sharp shark teeth that were so white they almost glowed. The deformed mouths made a chattering sound as they got close to the Leonidas. Holly, now wearing an armored suit shouted, "Third rank; fire!"

The line of operatives fired their rifles at once. All of them held down their triggers, only needing to point their muzzles down range to hit a target. The zombies' round, pumpkin heads rapidly split open as rounds flew through them. They fell by the hundred from the onslaught. The air stunk of burning rotten meat and molten rock from all the plasma rounds fired off. Despite the fire, the zombies kept coming, crushing their fallen under their bony feet. As the seven of them joined the line, they attached plasma bayonets to their muzzles. Calvin quickly checked his pistol over. It looked like they could be used as blunt instruments. Lane then smiled and said with glee in her voice, "What are you all waiting for? Let's join in!"

She flipped down her face mask as they joined in

the formation. The third rank fell back once their weapons over heated. Calvin and the others took their position as a part of the first rank. All of them took a knee and aimed their rifles at the upcoming horde. The zombies kept on dropping from the machine gun fire. Randomly the dead would get shredded by plasma. Sometimes their bodies would vaporize from the heat, leaving only a puddle of flesh behind. A volley of rockets flew overhead and detonated right over the horde. The shrapnel burst seemed to tear hundreds of them apart at once. Despite all the fire power, it was just slowing down the massive horde, not stopping them. Holly sounded off. "First rank…!"

Calvin aimed his rifle at the head of the first zombie that came across his sights and placed his finger on the trigger, "…fire!"

Everyone on the line fired at once. Calvin felt blinded as the muzzle flashes blurred his vision. He held down his trigger along with everyone else. The zombies in front of them were torn apart from the waist up. As they quickly fired, their weapons overheated. They fell back as the next rank started firing. Rose yelled, "How long is this supposed to hold them for?"

One of the other operatives told her, "Long enough for the ship's systems to come online!"

"How long could that take?" Dumont asked as the

next rank fell back. It was almost their turn again. The horde's loud moans and chattering teeth could still be heard over the weapons going off. It only seemed to get more intense as more of them crawled up to them. Their feet made a sickening squishing sound as they trampled over the re-killed bodies. With every group that fell, more took their place. A part of the mountain gave away in an avalanche. Massive amounts of dirt and rocks came sliding down into the horde. They were crushed under the torrent of earth. It bought enough time for everyone's rifles to cool off. It wasn't much. Some of the zombies survived and crawled out from the dirt. Calvin and his rank went up to the line and only needed to hear the word "Fire" before pulling back on the trigger. The weapons fire only stopped for a brief second before more rifles fired off. That's when they saw some of the zombies were able to run and dodge the rounds. The front rank quickly pulled out their side arms and fired as fast as they could yank back on their triggers. This bought enough time for the next rank to get in position. The ground started to shake from something other than the massive number of explosives being thrown at the horde. Beth asked, "Is that what I think it is?"

Three Claw Mechs charged up the mountain. They were covered in dead bodies and lots of blood. They made a disgusting sound with every step they took. The plain round head seemed to be cracked like a mirror. Rose shouted, "Those fuckers can pilot a Mech?"

"That's bullshit!" Valery shouted. Damon gasped, "Guess they had something... make that someone good to eat."

"We need bigger guns," Alan bluntly stated as the giants got closer to them.

Calvin suddenly felt the sensation that something was drawn to him. From out of one of the hangers a Titan came flying out. Without thinking, Calvin boosted up in the air towards the machine. Some of the zombies started leaping up at him as he flew. He fired back at them with his rifle. They fell back to the ground splattering on impact. His rifle overheated forcing him to switch to his pistol. The last one was almost within reach before he got pulled inside the Titan's cockpit. His vision and sensations transferred to that of the machines. He smiled, "This is fire power!"

Two weapons swung out into the machine's hands as every weapons system on the Titan fired off. Several hundred antipersonnel grenades flew over the horde and shredded them to bits. With a couple rounds from the torso and head mounted weapons, whole groups of zombies vanished in a flash. The operators started pulling back to the ship itself. Holly spoke up, "Hold them just a bit longer. The ship is almost good to go!"

"Will do!" He shouted with confidence. A back mounted cannon flipped over the Mech's shoulder and fired into the ground causing another landslide. It took most of the zombies with it. They got caught up in the dirt and mud as they were pulled back down the mountain. The giant Ghouls leaped over the falling rocks and dirt, keeping stride as they charged up the mountain. Calvin fired another round form the large cannon on the machine's back. The Claw machines managed to dodge the round. One of them even fired back taking the cannon off the Titan's back. Calvin ditched the damaged cannon and fired away with his machine's handheld weapons. The first Ghoul Mech burst apart and fell to pieces into the flowing dirt it was walking on. When the hand-held weapons overheated, two internal weapons popped out and fired rapidly at the next machine. It didn't seem to stop coming as he kept pumping rounds into the deformed Ghoul. He shot both the head and the torso. Only when the limbs flew off did it fall apart. The last one leaped forward taking a swipe at the Titan with its talons. Calvin had his machine pull his two plasma knives to block the sharp objects. They made a flash of light as the sharp blades impacted into one another. He moved back either dodging or deflecting every jab that came at him. The machine spun forward in the air and kicked Calvin's Titan down to the ground on its back. Calvin got a warning that the ship's weapons were now active again. The Ghoul leaped at Calvin with its arms side to side ready to swipe at him. He waited until the last moment before boosting out from under the enemy. The machine swiped its arms at the dirt as the ship vaporized the Mech in a single laser blast. The Leonidas rose up into the air with the dirt flying off the ship. She shined in the sun like a phoenix rising from the ashes. Calvin looked back down seeing the zombie horde coming back up the mountain with even more Ghoul Mechs coming up after them. He quickly rocketed up into the air and flew into one of the open hanger doors. They slammed shut in front of him once the Titan landed inside. He could still see images of the outside world. The ship fired several laser bursts and torpedoes down at the horde taking them out in massive explosions. Soon the only thing left of the mountain and city below were several mushroom clouds. He laughed to himself, "We are out of here!"

Holly told him, "Not yet."

"Shit!"

CHAPTER 17
CALM
LOW ORBIT OF EAGLE STABLE
S.I.S. LEONIDAS
CLASSROOM

CALVIN sat back on the chair looking up at the plan overhead feeling at ease for the first time in what felt like a long time. Yet he was still on edge knowing his plight wasn't over. The others were sitting around the room silent as they waited to see what they were going to do next. The door opened to the room and the six people they upgraded walked in. Everyone felt awkward as the door closed leaving them together. Lane spoke up first, "We were told to report to Alpha squad."

"Welcome," Calvin told them as they drifted in the room and sat down in the metal chairs. Valery stood up, "Okay we need to address what happened."

"Please no," Alan begged in vain. Damon suggested, "Why don't we exchange names first?"

"Cage," the man that was with Rose spoke up first. The woman that was with Alan spoke next, "Katlin."

"Tory," the woman that was with Damon said. The woman that was with Beth told them, "Rotten."

"Nice," Alan told him. The last man spoke up, "Greg. So, you all made us like your former lovers? Couldn't get over them or something, or were you drugged-up assholes just trying to smooth over your guilty conscience?"

"Yes, that. The first thing. Wait a second, we're impaired too! Fuck off!" Alan told him trying to hide his shame.

"Like this shit isn't jacked up enough as is," Rose grumbled to herself. Cage replied sarcastically, "Oh, you all were tricked into taking drugs and forcing yourselves on others? That's terrible!"

"Just following orders, right? Whatever helps your sick assholes sleep at night!" Rotten added. Damon was about to shout back at him then stopped and shrugged, "Fuck it. We're morally reprehensible anyway."

"Hate to ask, but do any of you remember who you were?" Beth wondered. All of them rocked their heads side to side. Alan asked, "So you remember being impaired?"

All six of them sighed with embarrassment. Lane spoke up first, "Yeah... never felt more terror in my life:

wondering when I would be able to eat, if I would wake up if I fell asleep, wondering if you all would hurt us. Guess we all know how that turned out."

"We were easily entertained by a laser pointer…" Cage told them, shaking his head.

"All of us should get our heads checked for going along with this," Calvin said with guilt in his voice. Lane added, "For what it's worth, we know none of you asked to be in that situation. A screwed-up silver lining as it may be, there was enough time to get the ship repaired. We'd be zombie meat if we hadn't been covered."

"I thought Holly was fucking with us when she said there was no other way," Valery grumbled in a defeatist tone. Rotten laughed, "What did you expect when we're built to kill and fuck, a simple handshake?"

"So how are all of you all variations of the same person again?" Troy asked trying to change the subject. Damon told her, "Well, when Calvin messed with the slip gate, he opened doors to other realties. Besides some DNA, we all have another thing in common! Our organizations wanted to get rid of us!"

"What's your story in your timeline?" Rose asked him. Valery shouted, "How about we save the bullshitting for when this is over? As in when we get the hell out of this system. Pardon me if I don't want to get attached. I've lost too many friends already."

"You're a cold one," Cage told her as they all looked to the doors as they opened. Rotten grumbled, "Here comes the witch."

Holly sighed as she closed the doors behind her and pulled off her helmet, "I can't be that predictable!"

"Lucky guess," Damon told her. She smirked, "So, did you all have fun? Was it really that bad? Oh wait, that's right! All of you were wusses that had to get doped up to get it up! You're welcome saving you all from death, again! Ungrateful pricks. Also, before you former grunts even think about crying about how you all got your marbles back, think about where you'd be if you didn't get the STI: throwing your poop around and looking at a laser like stupid animals."

None of them wanted to talk to her after that. They stared at her, waiting. She looked around the classroom, "That's what I thought. The whole future is ahead of us. Buck up. This wasn't the first time you've been forced into a jacked-up situation. Won't be the last. In fact, I'm about to send you all into one right now!"

Rotten shouted at her, "You suck!"

"Something tells me this isn't going to be an orgy this time," Greg grumbled. Holly pulled up an image of a massive underground complex, which showed a nuclear symbol "We need to blow this system up as soon as possible, and this island has just the item we need. Our Claw contact is holed up there, too."

"You want us to recuse her? She used us and that whore was going to have us all killed! Didn't you technically stab her in the back by making that third party deal that allegedly saved us?" Beth pointed out to her. Alan shouted, "Better idea, leave them for the zombies."

"Another question, why didn't we bring Nova Bombs of our own? Wouldn't it have been simpler to just blow up the system and blame the Vegans?" Cage asked. Holly laughed, "You wonder why I'm a hard ass to you all. No one would ever blow up their home system. Yes, there was the station drop and shit, but no sun busting. They just wanted a black eye; not a missing appendage to justify their war. I would love nothing more than to leave that asshole screamer to get eaten, but consider this. War has begun between a third faction with the Vegan remnant supporting them. The Claws are the only barrier we have between our system getting invaded out of retaliation. They get to expand, and we get power. Win, win for everyone... save the third party that my associate is screwing over."

"Oh, this is reassuring. How are the Vegans still even a threat?" Greg asked her. She replied, "They are quite resilient amphibians. Another thing you morons should think about; until we get our ace in the hole, we only have a handful of ships. The Claws still have almost a million. Any other questions you ask-holes?"

Tory lifted her hand up into the air and asked, "What would you call a handful of ships number wise?"

"Only five other ships are functional. To top things off, not all of them will survive the next few hours." She showed them battle footage of the destroyers on the run from a several other vessels that looked like they were created from wreckage. Some of them looked like Spartan ships. One of them took the combined fire power of five of the ships to destroy it in a massive ball of fire. The images vanished and were replaced with the island again. "Those zombies have evolved to the point where they can fly a ship. We can't let them leave this system. Only one surefire way to assure that. I'll give you all a hint. It involves a ball of fire and making it go boom!"

She focused the images of the complex and showed just how massive it was. The structure was large enough for a Mech to maneuver around inside easily. In fact, "Only way we're going to get the Nova Bomb out of there is with Titans. Maneuvering will be tight. You'll only bring the light weapons and won't be able to have heavy armor either. The other squads will keep the perimeter clear. Just need to get in, get the bomb and the Claw operative and get out. Easy day for once!"

"I don't believe you. Wait a second. Do you know if other systems have a zombie infestation, too?" Lane asked. Holly told her, "The third party only had two prototype weapons, and seeing how things turned out here, I don't think they'll mass produce them."

"Ma'am, any idea on how many zombies we'll have to deal with?" Beth asked. Holly replied, "We don't know. Assume it's going to be a lot of bastards down there. They had a lot to eat, so they're going to be hard to kill. Time waits for no one. Get to your Titans and prep for drop."

"Like we have a choice," Calvin told her sarcastically. She laughed, "You all chose to be here from one decision in your lives. I think you all know which one I'm talking about. Now get going, douche bags."

She opened the door and motioned for them all to get out. They got up and started to fill out into the passageway. As they did, Rose asked Beth, "So in your memories you hooked up with Duncan?"

"We were bored and figured why not?" She told her quickly. Damon laughed, "He's going to get a laugh out of this!"

Calvin asked, "Lane, just wondering, do any of you have our memories or the memories of the people we've been with?"

Lane thought about it, "We are what you perceived your lovers to be like. I should be lucky that you thought of Jane so well."

"Wait, how do you know about that?" He asked nervously. She told him, "You kept saying her name in your sleep. Don't lose your resolve now. I want to see Earth and Mars again, too, in the case of me and the former grunts, for the first time."

"First time for everything." He rubbed his head. She smiled, "We're on an alien planet that is infested with cybernetic zombies and we need to blow up the nearby star. Weird is the new normal. Abnormal if you will!"

"That's just a matter of perspective," Rotten told her. They all started making their way to the armory. Calvin smiled, "We can get even with the assholes that sent us to die!"

"You hold them down, and I'll punch!" Cage told him as they started laughing at the idea. As they moved along they got quiet again. The ship's alarms sounded off again as the crew got ready for another fire. Calvin breathed and thought to himself, "What would I do if I saw you again, Jane?"

CHAPTER 18
EAGLE STABLE
S.I.S. LEONIDAS
HANGER BAY

CALVIN tapped his Titan's fingers against the cannon it carried. An image popped up of the island they were coming up on. They codenamed it 'Easter Egg Island.' Several torpedoes flew from the ship and exploded over the island. The flash blinded the cameras for a solid minute straight. When the light faded, Calvin could see mushroom clouds and blue flashes of light rising from the patch of land. The blast caused a tsunami to form in the ocean. All the green and red vegetation was vaporized in an instant. The buildings were smashed and splattered to the ground. The once sunny day turned into a cloudy one as the black smoke blocked the sun. The Leonidas flew to the only standing structure left on the island. The bunker was covered in grass and dirt. It was the highest structure in the area. Surprisingly, its managed to withstand the explosions, with all the plants and houses nearby still intact as well. A countdown appeared on Calvin's HUD. Once it hit zero, he and the others leaped from the ship. Their boosters gave them a smooth landing as the giant feet of the Titans touched down on the ground. Calvin got carried away and did a roll when he hit the surface. No one seemed to care as they focused all their attention on the large doors in front of them. The Mechs formed a semicircle around the main bunker and aimed their weapons at the metal double doors. Valery asked, "Why do we have to open the door? We all know it's going to have zombies on the other side."

Greg pointed out, "Better question, why are we all aiming heavy weapons at a bunker filled with enough explosives to blow this planet up at least a hundred times over?"

Alan told him, "It survived a torpedo. I think it would survive our plasma cannons."

"How about this: how did we get so unlucky to get sent on a suicide mission in the first place?" Tory wondered out loud.

"Fuck us. That's why. In more ways than one..." Rotten told them with brutal honesty. Calvin spoke up, "Enough! We survived a suicide mission we weren't supposed to come back from the fucking zombie apocalypse! Don't wuss out now! Open the doors! We're the ones knocking this time!"

Damon and Katlin both cut the security locks off the doors and quickly stepped aside. Beth and Greg got on each side of the massive swinging double doors and stuck their knives into the middle. They both applied enough force to rip the doors open. There was a loud snap that went through the air as the doors parted from each other. The two of them quickly moved out of the line of fire as everyone was just about to pull their triggers. Suddenly a lone Claw ran out waving a white flag. Calvin shouted, "Hold fire!"

Several rounds went over the bunker as he shouted the order. The Claw started yelling at them. Valery asked, "This is ironic… I think. A person who caused a false flag is now waving a flag of distress. What's she saying?"

"I'm guessing, 'Oh, I didn't think you'd all make it. No hard feelings about almost getting you all killed. Right?' if I had to guess," Greg laughed at his own joke. Calvin opened his tech and dropped his Titan to his knee. He grabbed a rifle and hopped out to face the survivor. Holly came over the comm, "Do not shoot her!"

"Relax! I'm leaving my comfort zone of violence and trying to explore the unpleasantness of diplomacy," he told her as he walked towards the Claw operative. She got close enough to him where they could hear each other clearly. She grumbled at the sight of him, "You have got to be fucking kidding me."

"I could say the same about you still being alive," he told her. She made a gesture for Calvin to remove his helmet. He pulled back on it and let it hang from his neck. "Got to give you all credit," she said, "Didn't think you'd live long enough to have to deal with the zombies or the pulse."

"Thanks, I guess. Sorry your plans went tits up," Calvin told her sarcastically. She laughed bitterly, "Let's cut the bullshit. Shall we? You're here for the Nova Bombs. Right?"

"As much as I hate to say it, you too. Why Holly thinks you're trustworthy is beyond me," he tapped his fingers on the rifle as they both stared each other down. She started laughing again, showing off her sharp jagged teeth, "Because she knows that my death will cause your system to get its shit packed in. I'm your only chance at not getting invaded by the Vegans and the opportunistic fuckers that did this to us. Be thankful we're in the same boat for now."

"Trust me when I say I'm counting my blessings, too. You never gave me your name. Care to share one?" he asked her while keeping a straight face. Calvin struggled not to grin at his omission. "I'll go by Irene. Neither one of us took the time to learn each other's languages. Translators are much simpler."

"We all tend to take the easy way out," he stated with a smile. Irene laughed again, "Would have been easier to just knock on the door. Yet again, both of us expected the other to be dead. Now, first things last, you want a Nova Bomb. Don't you?" she guessed correctly. He nodded as he grumbled, "Oh, for fuck's sake! You know this already, and you said you'd cut the bullshit! You're sounding just like Yosemite!"

"Don't compare me to him! He's dead. That favor you did me will only get you so far. In the meantime, I'll tell you how to get to the bomb if you get me off this planet, but you have to get the nine hundred fifty-four people who made it to the bunker as well. I also want your race's help in fighting the fuckers who sucker punched us! It's the only way to ensure you won't get blamed for what occurred," Irene told him bluntly.

"Blackmailing us for support?" he asked her as he tried not to laugh. "I prefer extortion. I wouldn't waste time with you all if I didn't think you weren't worthy assets, seeing how you survived the impossible."

"We try. I'm in if you are," Calvin took a couple steps forward while releasing his rifle as it slammed into his chest. He offered his hand to her. Irene nodded and grabbed his hand. They rocked them up and down quickly once and separated. "This could be the start of a beautiful... acquaintance-ship."

"I guess that's the best the two of us can hope for," Calvin smiled at her, "Yes."

"Moving on, I suggest you all bring your own food and airtight suits. Our stuff probably won't be compatible with your biology," he told her as she laughed, "I'll worry about the survivors. You worry about getting past all the zombies and procuring the bomb."

Irene made a motion for the others to come out. Calvin quickly got on the comm link. "Hold fire. Non-hostiles coming out," he told the others they appeared. There was a long stream of people that moved out of the bunker. They had on tattered clothing and all looked scared out of their minds. All of them were shorter than their military counterparts with smaller limbs as well. Their fears weren't eased by the Titans looming over them. Calvin could have sworn he saw the same kid that shot him in the head. He shrugged off the feeling and got on the comm link again, "We're going to need transports to get the civilians out of here."

"I heard the conversation. Nice job by the way," Holly told him. He laughed, "I know. I followed your orders. How could I disobey?"

"You can't. While the Leonidas gets all the survivors on board, head in and get the bomb. Irene has just transmitted the codes for you all to get past security. Just to let you know, we're also going to need most of our operators onboard to make sure nothing funny happens. To top that off, the Leonidas is going to high tail it once we get the survivors on board," Holly told them. Calvin looked up at the ship, "Leaving us to rot like the Spartans did?"

"Chill out. Go in and get your golden ticket for a ride off this rock. Get the bomb and be ready to fly in an hour's time. The Agis Three will only pick you all up if the bomb is yours. Good luck."

"You, too," he told her as the link went dead. The transports came down and loaded up all the civilians, bringing them up by groups to the ship. Several of the operatives also headed up themselves. Irene got on the comm link, "Your command is only leaving twelve of you to get the bomb and get out?"

"Yeah. If you have information, don't be selfish. Share. I don't think you want this zombie infestation leaving the system either," Calvin told her. He heard another laugh. "There's at least one hundred forty-six operational Thins in there. The zombies had plenty to eat, so they're going to know how to pilot them. Plus, there at least ten thousand regular zombies to worry about as well."

"Good job with your screening process on who got in! How large is the complex?" Calvin wondered after his sarcastic outburst. "You'll see it soon enough. Can you pull another miracle out of your asses, or was that a onetime thing?"

"Deus ex Machina works in mysterious ways, or at least that's what we're told," he replied to her looking at the open doors with dread. "Don't let that bullshit go to your heads. Good luck, for what it's worth."

The line went dead. Calvin let out a long grumble as he walked back to his Titan. He boosted up into the air and flew backwards into the cockpit. Once he was back in control, the other eleven walked up behind him. Greg asked, "So we're getting ditched and our only chance is to get a bomb that can kill a star?"

"Yeah, fuck us. Right? Keep your shields charged and use your anti-personnel grenades sparingly. Save the heavy weapons for the enemy Ghouls. Don't forget to double tap," he told them as they all made their way inside the bunker. It really was huge. It was large enough for all twelve of their Titans to walk side by side without bumping into each other. There seemed to be a massive lift in front of them that went down diagonally, an officer structure to one side and a bay of handling equipment to the other. It was well illuminated, showing the nonskid deck, cranes, and storage crates. The ceiling showed a bright and sunny day up above. Tory asked, "Why can't we ever go anyplace nice?"

"Where's the fun in that?" Rotten asked. Once all twelve of them were on the lift, Calvin ordered, "Greg, put the lift into free fall. Once it looks like we're about to hit bottom, everyone boost-up and shoot everything in sight. Understand?"

"I don't want to," Beth told him. Greg went over to the controls and sighed, "Let's have a nice trip and live to see next fall."

The lift fell out from under them. All of them were practically in a free fall as they slid downwards. Their Titans skidded on the metal sending sparks flying. The further they got down, they started to see a massive green environment below them. It had grass and even multiple pools of water. The outer edges were holographic images showing similar scenery and a regular purple sky. As they got closer, they saw the zombies start moving towards the lift. Along the outer edges, doors were slammed open as deformed Ghouls came stumbling out into the open. Each one of them looked like they placed spare parts on themselves and carved faces into their plain round heads. Their numbers rapidly started to grow as they filed out into the open. Everyone either said, "Shit" or "Fuck" out of dread. The ground came up rapidly, "Boost!"

All twelve of them flew up into the air as the lift slammed down violently into the ground. It sent ripples through the dirt and knocked the zombies off their feet. The boom echoed in the space loudly as the enemy Ghouls went into a full sprint towards them. A door illuminated in their HUDs showing them where they needed to go. It was also the source of the oncoming Mechs. The zombies and their machines followed them as they got lower and lower to the ground. Calvin ordered, "Hold fire! Form an echelon formation when we land!"

"Couldn't we just stay in the air?" Damon asked as an indicator went off showing they'd have to land. Calvin grumbled, "If only."

They were almost within arm's reach of the enemy machines as they swiped up at them with their sharp talons. One in front of them leaped up into the air and flew at them, "Fire!"

Everyone did so at once. The enemy Giants in front of them were knocked down after multiple rounds passed through them. When the team hit the ground, they went into a sprint. Their Titans moved their legs and stretched, adding some boost to their movement to go faster. They also swung their arms around firing as fast as their weapons could put rounds down range. The shrapnel rounds took out hundreds of zombies at once in a rain of molten metal. Their bodies burned and fell apart from the heat. Once the Titan's energy was recharged, Calvin shouted, "Boost!"

All of them flew up into the air. They landed in the only clearing they had. A loud scream pierced through their comm link. Alan's Titan was impaled and being dragged into the swarm. Rose screamed, "No!"

She rapidly fired multiple rounds at the horde creating massive craters. A hailstorm of body parts came back down. His large weapons sliced three Ghouls. They blew up when they hit the surface, but it wasn't enough. The zombies were like ants in a frenzy as they leaped onto his machine. Most of them exploded against the energy shield. Yet, once it popped, they were all over the Titan. His machine pulled out his knife, and he started stabbing every Ghoul that came up to him. He also slammed his limbs together to crush the climbing zombies. He shouted, "Do me a favor and burn this system!"

"We're not…!" Rose got cut off, by Calvin, "Go out with a bang!"

The team reluctantly kept going, leaving Alan as he fought with everything he had. He took down five more machines before the zombies ripped open his cockpit. He came out guns blazing. He aimed two massive machine guns, one to both of his sides and took down zombies by the dozens. Their bodies burned upon being hit and disintegrated. It wasn't enough to stop them. He suddenly got bitten multiple times. He lifted up a grenade and shouted in pain, "Choke on this!"

The explosion managed to take out all the zombies and seven Ghouls in a gigantic plume of ashes and debris. The rest of the team came upon the entrance they had enter. They were knocking down multiple Ghouls with their concentrated blast. The Giants fell back with massive burning holes in their torsos. The grenades flew up from the Titan's feet and exploded in midair above the zombie hordes. They vanished into small burning shards right afterwards. They left a trail of re-dead remnants behind them. The entrance was suddenly blocked by one Ghoul that was covered in green blood. It lifted one of its arms and fired. Rose got hit, "Fucking bullshit!"

She then flew forward firing away at the enemy Titan. She got hit three more times before she crashed into the machine. She pushed all the Giants back single handedly as her Titan got stabbed repeatedly. She fired back with her torso and head mounted weapons to slow them down. Rose pushed her boosters to the limit and blew them out as she cleared a path for the rest of the team.

She shouted, "Burn those fuckers!"

They ran past her as her Titan was ripped apart. It self-destructed, cutting the enemy Mechs in half. Their torsos burst open, sending a torrent of metal gushing out. Calvin shouted enraged, "Fucking damn it!"

"They'll be fucking avenged," Valery told him as they moved through a tunnel. Greg and Tory took point shooting the halved Ghouls. Both fearlessly charged forward clearing the way. Tory suddenly took multiple hits. The zombies now knew how a trigger worked. Tory got in front of Greg and used herself as a shield while he fired back at the enemy. "I'll get mine!" Tory shouted as she did a kamikaze. She flew right into a group of Ghouls. The explosion sent them crashing into the ground. They all went flat from the force of the blast. Calvin shouted in frustration, "How the fuck much further do we need to go?"

"We're almost there! Just hold on a little longer!" Valery told him. Behind them, the swarm followed. They even fired pot shots at them trying to slow their movement down. Valery fired several rounds into the ceiling above them. Lane shouted, "Stop! You're going to cause a cave in!"

"That's the damned idea!" she snapped back.

"There is no other way out, dip-shit!" she shouted

back at her. Katlin shouted, "That's crap!"

"Stop being a wuss!" Valery shouted as they came upon the massive doors. Greg told them, "Hold them off. I need to enter in the codes!"

Now you must be kidding us!" Damon shouted at him as they formed a firing line in front of the door. Calvin shouted. "Hell, just fucking cause the cave in!"

"Don't think it's going to hold them for long," Rotten said as the rocks started to slam into to the floor in front of them. Lane shouted, "Just needs to be long enough!"

Everyone fired up at the ceiling causing whole sections of concrete, dirt and metal to drop down on top of the zombie horde. The Ghouls were only able to come at them piecemeal. The group fired in bursts tearing apart the machines as they came through. They kept firing waves of grenades at the zombies. They started forming a massive puddle of blood, guts, bones, and oil on the ground as they kept getting ripped apart. Calvin asked, "How much longer, damn it!"

"Fucking got it!" He shouted as the doors came open. There were several massive doors that slid to the side bit by bit. Greg reached in and gently pulled out the bomb. In this case it was torpedo, "That's it?"

"Unless that fucking lizard was pulling a joke, I

think this is it. Let's get the flying hell out of here!" He shouted as they all moved forward. Suddenly, the whole ceiling came down on top of them. They all moved as one group to avoid being smashed by the heavy rocks. Lane shouted, "Can't we make our own way out?"

"Just might work!" Rotten shouted as he pointed out a spot ahead of them, "Throw every heavy explosive you guys got at that spot. Then fly through it!"

All of them did so. They threw all the grenades they had at the opening. The grenades detonated upon impact. Light came through the rupture as all of them rocketed up through the breach. Damon, Beth and Katlin were the first ones through and quickly screamed, "Look out!"

The others stopped just short of hitting the ground. Katlin and Beth were able to fly back up while Damon got swarmed by several Ghouls and foot zombies. He shouted, "Oh, just go!"

They flew over him as he set his Titan to self-destruct. The blast sent metal, body parts, and dirt up into the air. The dome shaped ceiling above them started to crack and fall apart. Massive sections came down on top of them. As they scrambled to get back to the lift, all the lights went off along with the holo projections. They switched back to night vision. They were running head long into a pack of machines that were rushing towards them. They quickly leaped over and fired off several rockets at them. All of them except Greg made it to the other side. He got dragged down. He threw the Nova Torpedo like a football, "Catch it!"

Valery went into the air while the others covered her. She grabbed it and kicked the Ghoul that tried to attack her and used the force to fly back to the team. Once she landed, Greg's machine exploded after being impaled multiple times. Calvin's body was shaking in shock and anger. He dropped his two external weapons and had his internal arm cannon pop up. His mechanical hand grabbed the two plasma knives as he charged forward. He fired twice, getting fatal hits on the Ghouls. As he dropped to the ground, he leaped on top of them and used them to jump forward. He stabbed two more Ghouls in the torso, let go and fired to his sides with his cannons. He hit them fast, enough to where all dropped at once after being hit. He fired off his torso and head mounted weapons, knocking down another five enemy machines. They spewed from the plasma punching into their metal frames. He ducked down, dodging the talons of a Ghoul strike. Valery and Beth shot down the two machines. Calvin rolled forward, using his knives to lift up the two damaged machines and threw them forward, knocking down multiple deformed Mechs in front of them. He quickly put away one of his knives and pulled out a massive cannon from his Titan's lower back. With his machine's right arm, he fired the cannon, ripping six Ghouls to shards in a split second. Calvin's left arm kept firing small bursts. They mowed their way through the horde as the dome started to completely collapse on top of them. Beth let out a yelp as her machine got cut in half by a falling piece of debris. The rest of her machine got smashed in by the rocks. Calvin shouted, "No!"

Beth managed to eject and was flying toward them. Rotten went back and got her. He caught her in his machine's arms as dust filled the air. The team came upon the slope and boosted their way up. None of the foot zombies could follow them. The Ghouls on the other hand were hot on their heels. Between each boost, they would fire a salvo knocking the Mechs back down. Valery and Rotten started blasting away at the ceiling behind them. The metal crushed the machines like bugs. They made it up to the top quickly and scrambled as the ground started to give away under them. All of them rushed out of the bunker as the whole island was collapsing in on itself. Water started to sweep across the land and dump into the cracks. From said cracks, a mechanical hand reached up. Rotten shouted, "Assholes aren't totally dead yet?"

From above came a loud bomb and a flash as the Spartan destroyers came through the clouds. Behind them, several zombie-piloted ships followed. Calvin yelled, "Boost!"

They all went into the air as massive waves of water came at them. Katlin was suddenly impaled by a set of talons and went back down, "No! Fuckers!"

She exploded when she was attacked by the Ghouls from below. They just managed to dodge the liquid as it covered the whole island. The Agis Three came flying down and opened its doors. Inside, the netting popped up and the crew got ready for them to land. It came at them like a bullet. Calvin and Valery caught the inside. Rotten, Lane and Beth held on for dear life. Calvin went forward and pulled them all inside before the doors closed. The net gave way and they all went flying into the bulkhead with a violent slam.

CHAPTER 19
HOME STRETCH
DATE UNKNOWN
ORBIT OF EAGLE STABLE
S.I.S. AGIS THREE
HANGER BAY

CALVIN opened his eyes. He felt his machine. It was still intact. The cockpit echoed with a scream of rage and sorrow. Valery patted his Titan's shoulder, "We fucking made it! Almost done!"

"Let's help them load up that explosive bastard!" he shouted as he got out of the Titan's cockpit. The others followed him as they ran over to Valery's machine. Her Mech's hand grabbed the torpedo and moved it over to them. She asked, "I know it's late, but is this type of ammunition compatible with your weapons systems?"

"Shit!" All of them shouted at once. Rotten asked, "Why didn't we think of that earlier?"

"We just need to get the damned torpedo to the

star. We'll throw it in there if we have to!" Calvin shouted. The ship rocked violently. Beth shouted, "You've got to be fucking kidding me!"

"That's life," Rotten grumbled as they got hit again. Calvin got on the comm, "Bridge, is there any way we can shake these fuckers off?"

"What the hell do you think we've been trying to do?" an angry voice shouted at him. "Is there anything we can do?"

"Don't get in the way!" The ship rocked again. Calvin looked up at the others, "I know we've been asked to do a lot, but think we could try taking back one of our ships?"

"Priorities! We need to get this fucking bomb," Valery answered.

"Torpedo," Rotten told her. "What the hell ever! Get this explosive thing to the damn sun! Now!" Valery pointed out, showing her anxiety. "We fucking will! Bridge!" he shouted. "What?"

"Send anyone that's available to the hanger bay! We're going to take back one of our destroyers! We'll also bring the bomb with us. Lead the enemy on a goose chase! Once they break off, make a run for it!"

"Fuck it! Fine. Good luck! Only blow up the sun and not the job!" she told him. "Same to you!"

"What does that mean?" Lane asked him as he huffed, "Just get back in your Titan!"

He flew back to his machine as the personnel came in. There were only sixty. Thankfully, they were all converted and had on armored suits. The lot of them all piled into a single Crain transport. Calvin and the others had their Titans move to the hanger bay doors. He brought up images of the zombie-controlled ships. "We're going for the Jason. She's the least damaged and the closest. It's going to be a rough landing! Once we get onboard, double kill everything that still moves!"

"Fuck yeah!" He heard shouted over the comm.

The doors opened and everyone flew out into the vacuum of space. The Agis Three fired several rounds at the zombie destroyers to give enough cover for them to slip in. The Tri-Star shaped ship got bigger quickly. They flew past a hole in their energy shields and blasted a hole into their hanger bay. They all rushed in at once. Calvin, Valery, Lane, Beth, and Rotten fired every anti-personnel grenade they had left in their suits. It ripped apart the zombies in the hanger instantly. Their blood and metal splattered on the bulkhead and deck. The Titans quickly stabbed the zombie-controlled Mechs before they could react. The Crain landed and the breach behind them was sealed. The operators came flying out finishing the remaining zombies. "Clear!"

"All fucking clear! Set the Titans to sentry mode! Have ten operators stay here and keep guard of the bomb... I mean torpedo! Everyone else, sweep the ship! Shoot everything!" Calvin shouted as he leaped out of his machine. He pulled a pulse shotgun from his back and gave it a charge with a pump of the slide.

"Fine by us!" The other operators lined up next to the doors and got ready to breach. "We go for the bridge! Once there, we can activate the auto turrets and other security systems to re-kill the rest of the fuck-heads on this ship!"

He got right in front of the door and rocketed towards it, "On me!"

Calvin stopped just shy of the metal door. He saw several zombies on the other side through a porthole. He stuck his shotgun at the glass window and fired. Then he threw a grenade though the hole and ducked back behind the corner. The blast sent what was left of the door flying across the hanger bay. Calvin rushed around the corner and fired again, finishing the zombies in the airlock. The other door opened with a hiss as more of them came after him. He pulled out his arm mounted pistol, shooting seven more zombies in the head as he recharged his shotgun with a pump of the slide. Another blast cut apart eight zombies.

The others fired with their rifles. The zombies went down by the dozens from the plasma rounds. Calvin rocketed forward. Using his body as a battery ram, he shoved a massed group of them into each other. He ducked out of the way as grenades flew into them and exploded. They splattered against the passageway, painting it with their blood. Calvin rushed to a lift and started to force the door open. From the crack came several zombie arms reaching out for him. One blast from his shot gun blew off all the limbs. He let the shotgun float in the air and he rapidly fired away with his arm mounted weapons. The tops of their heads ripped off with each round that hit them. Valery slapped him on the back, "They're re-fucking-killed! Let's go!"

They cut a hole into the bottom of the lift and rocketed down the shaft. Calvin went down first. He crashed through the double doors and knocked down several zombies that were waiting for him. He threw a grenade to one side and fired off his shotgun to the other. The others quickly followed him in. Calvin didn't even wait for the rest of the zombies to get cleared out before he crashed through the door to the bridge. There was only one zombie there. It was another replicate of Valery. She gave him a smile as she pulled out two plasma knives. "Wondering when I would get a real challenge."

Calvin fired his shotgun. The zombie dodged the blast and threw one of the knives hitting the shotgun. He threw the damaged weapons aside and blocked the jabs as the came at him. The zombie suddenly had spikes coming out of its elbows, knees and feet. It made stabbing motions with all eight blades. Calvin blocked the two handheld knives, but the zombie moved her body right up to him and bit his face mask off. He swung his hand downwards and cut off both of the zombie's arms and kicked her against the bulkhead. He laughed, "Should have gone for the head!"

The two arms flew back and reattached themselves to the zombie. Rotten asked, "Need help?"

"Shoot her!"

They all fired at the zombie. She managed to dodge all the round and got right back up close to Calvin. The others held fire unable to get a clear shot. The elbow and knee knives flew out of her. Calvin was able to deflect two and dodge one blade. The last one however got him right in the stomach. He bent forward and got stabbed twice more by the foot mounted knives in the torso. The zombie thrust her knives down at Calvin's head. Valery blocked the stab and kicked her counterpart in the head. Both swung at each other with their blades. They both went from side to side pushing against each other. The zombie managed to pin Valery to the bulkhead. Calvin threw both his knives at the zombie, cutting its arms again. Valery cut the zombie's legs off. Calvin pulled the knife lodged in his stomach out and boosted towards the two of them. Both Valery and Calvin stabbed the zombie in the head at the same time as it let out a screech. To be safe, they shoved an incendiary grenade to the zombie and threw her out into the passageway where she burned. Rotten and Lane shot the zombie over and over to make sure it would stay dead. Valery moaned, "That fucking hurt!"

"Tell me about it! Rotten! Lane! Get this bastard back on our team!" he ordered. The two of them quickly activated all the security systems on the ship. Images popped up of the zombies getting cleared out by auto turrets, vented into space, burned by force fields, smashed by gravitational control and even dissolved by environmental systems. The images shifted over the other zombie-controlled ships as they chased after their friends. Calvin yelled, "Rotten, can you hack their systems and lower their shields?"

"Done!" he said with a grin. "Lucky us! Full spread of torpedoes!" He pointed forward in triumph as the blue balls of light flew to their targets. The blast stopped all the ships in their tracks. The remaining five friendly ships fired back finishing them off. Every one of the zombie ships was ripped apart in a sphere of flames and flying metal. There was a cheer in the bridge when a large fragment from one of the destroyed ships came flying at them. Beth shouted, "Incoming!"

CHAPTER 20
STARBURST
DATE UNKNOWN
S.I.S. JASON
BRIDGE

CALVIN was slapped in the face, forcing him to wake up. He quickly got up and saw they were heading right for the red sun. Beth was at the controls with several spikes of metal sticking out of her. She was also next to three dozen dead zombies. Calvin asked, "Are you okay?"

She laughed bitterly as she showed him the bite marks, "What do you think?"

"No! We can fix you! This isn't fair! How much longer..." He asked while she pulled a pistol on her head. "What's more human than self-sacrifice?" She asked him with a tear going down her cheek, "I wish you could have seen me. It was a hell of a fight. One to remember!"

"Don't!" He shouted at her as she smiled, "Finish the job."

With a pull of the trigger, she fell sideways onto

the deck with a hole in in her head that let out a plume of steam. Rotten was screaming in sock. He rushed up to her body and held her, "No!"

Soon all of them were blinded by the sun light. It encompassed their whole view as they got closer and closer to the massive star. Rotten shouted as he gently closed Beth's eyes; "We got one last problem besides having to get the Nova... Torpedo into the sun."

"Doesn't sound as cool as bomb doesn't it?" Lane grumbled.

Valery shouted, "We got contact!" An image was brought up of an unknown ship. It was diamond-shaped and shimmered in the light. "Is it hostile?"

Lane got on a control console and told him, "Yes. It took a couple pot shots at us as we were making our run. Those fuckers managed to fuck up what weapon systems we had left."

Valery guessed, "If I didn't know any better, I'd say that those assholes want us to do a kamikaze."

"That would explain why they didn't blow us up," Rotten sighed. Calvin asked, "What about the rest of the battle group?"

"They're long gone. Safe and sound, unlike us!" Lane told him as the ship started rocking the closer they got to the sun. Calvin looked forward and came up with something, "Can we go to warp right now?"

"Yeah. I'm surprised how those zombies were able to make repairs. Got something in mind?" Rotten asked. Valery's eyes went wide, "You're going to use the sun to slingshot us into the enemy ship."

"I thought we were trying to avoid a fucking kamikaze?" Lane asked. He went on, "Not if our shields are at maximum and we're going as fast as we can without flying apart. Tell the operators still in the hanger bay to eject the torpedo when I give the word!"

"Is it even possible to activate the damned torpedo without it being in a tube?" Valery asked. Rotten answered, "Yes. I can rig something up. Just say when."

"Pyromaniac suddenly?" Lane asked him with a smile. "Don't worry about my fetishes! Put us on a path, and put us at full speed!"

"We're going to have to divert energy from places," Valery warned him. "Then we'd better get strapped in."

All of them strapped themselves into the chairs as the ship's shields glowed from the energy given off by the sun. Rotten hightailed it to the hanger as Lane asked, "Isn't the whole point of the Icarus story to not fly close to the sun?"

"Got to risk it to win it! I'm not losing anyone else! This is not the end! We're going to live to see the assholes who fucked us suffer! Now punch it!" Calvin shouted, emboldened as the ship turned and started its lap around the sun. All of them were being pushed against their seats as the ship moved faster. The temperature inside rose as well. The sun looked like an ocean of fire. The flames kept reaching out into space as the star burned. They had to move side to side to avoid the flares that came up. "Come on! Hold!"

Rotten came over the comm, "The torpedo is as ready as it's going to get! Just say when! It's really fucking hot!"

"No shit! We're right next to a star! Hold on!" he shouted as the heat was getting to him. They all felt like they were in an oven. They came around and saw the diamond-shaped ship in front of them. "When I give the word, fire the torpedo. Right after, warp."

Several of the images started to static as the hull sounded like it was buckling from the heat. He gasped, "Now!"

The torpedo fired off and sped towards the sun. It didn't take long before it went into the massive ball of energy. Everyone was suddenly pushed back against their chairs as the ship went to warp. The enemy ship rapidly grew. They didn't stop moving as they crashed through the massive vessel. They burst right through their shields and crashed through their hull like it was nothing. Right after they flew through the vessel, it exploded. The star behind them went dark. The temperature dropped quickly. The star let out a pulse as a shockwave ripped throughout the system. One by one, the planets were smashed against the wave of energy. They cracked open like eggs. Their outer shell would crack and break up into large fragments before the core of the world burst open sending molten rock into space, mixing in with the dirt and the frozen water. No planet in the system was spared. The system got smaller and smaller the further they got away. Soon there was a flash like none of them had ever seen. It seemed to be a massive burst of light in every color. It dispersed out like a cloud as it expanded behind them. Everyone seemed to ease up the further they got from that system. They took off the straps that were holding them down and let themselves drift up. The doors to the bridge opened and augmented crewmen started filing in. "All yours. Just take us to the link up point." The three of them of them left as the crewmen took over. Once they were outside the bridge, Calvin collapsed onto the deck, letting out a long moan. Valery came up behind him along with Lane. "You're all right."

He lifted a finger up, "I need a moment."

Rotten's voice came over the comm link, "Sorry,

but you're going to want to come to the hanger right now!"

The three of them looked at each other. Calvin got back up and started moving towards the hanger. The three of them went flying through the passageways and slammed open the doors as Rotten's Mech placed a small pod in the center of the hanger bay. All the operators were standing around it with their rifles aimed at the metal pod. It was a metallic color and it seemed to float in the air. Lane asked, "What the hell is that? And how did it survive?"

"We think it's an escape pod from that ship. It got caught in the hanger bay after we crashed into the enemy vessel. It's a sturdy bastard," Rotten told them. Valery asked, "Why did you all think it was a good idea to bring it onboard?"

He told them, "This might be the fucker responsible for the pulse! We can wring the person for information!"

"How thorough were your scans?" Lane asked him. He told her, "We scanned this bastard multiple times. All the reading is telling us is that there's a life form in there."

"Could this thing be a bomb or a trap?" Calvin asked. Rotten scanned the pod again, "No. Nothing explosive about this. Just a survival pod."

Calvin took a couple steps towards the object. "Can it be opened?"

"Yes…" Rotten said nervously. Calvin ordered, "Everyone, stand by."

All the operators and even the Mechs aimed their weapons at the pod. Calvin strapped a line around himself and told the others, "Pressurize the hanger. Get some clean air in here. Also restore gravity. Have someone get full body restraints and sedatives of…every kind. If anything happens, pull me back."

They nodded as they started giving out slack. He walked towards the pod as everyone less kept a distance. Calvin removed his helmet and let it dangle from his neck as the air rushed back in. His feet dropped down to the deck. Valery asked loudly, "What are you doing?"

"Showing this fucker who they're dealing with. Now stand by." He got up close to the pod. He saw the lines where the hatch would be and saw where the pod would be opened at. He quickly reached down, pushed the button and pulled his hand back. Both his arm mounted pistols were ready if he needed them along with his knives. The hatch swung open. A fog came out and blocked his view. He stepped back far enough where he wasn't caught up in it. He almost flipped his helmet back on when he saw a shape of the thing inside. The smoke cleared, he moved back up to the pod and looked down. "What the fuck?"

"What is it?" Valery shouted in anticipation. Everyone lifted their rifles up and leaned forward onto the balls of their feet. Calvin reached over the figure and snapped his fingers. The woman opened her eyes. She looked human. She had white hair, pale skin and a black and blue suit that covered most of her body. Her head seemed slightly larger than a human and her eyes were large and round. She only had four fingers on her hands and four toes on her feet. Other than that, she looked almost identical to anyone else. Her large eyes looked over to him. He told her, "My name is Calvin Marley of... formerly of Sparta Corps. Who are you? Do you understand what I'm saying?"

She nodded. "Good. Are you going to talk?"

She nodded again. "Now is as good a time as any. Who are you?"

She said nothing. "Fine. Now either you can cooperate, or we can have you put into restraints and sedated. If you would, kindly step out of the pod."

The woman got up and hopped out of the pod. She stood only five feet five, much shorter than the average seven feet that everyone else was. Calvin motioned for a couple operators to move up. "Rotten, jettison the pod. Put some explosives in there and blow it up. As for you," he looked at the woman as she kept staring up at him. "Have anything to say?"

She stood there silently smiling at him. Calvin sighed, "Okay."

He motioned for two operators to go over and guard her. He motioned to another two to come to him. He talked quietly, "Take her someplace secure and watch her like a hawk. Do not let her out of your sight for even a second. If she does anything, let me know. Don't say anything to her. She only talks to me. If she acts up, use tranquilizers on her or knock her out with…"

"Petty officer, we'll take every fucking precaution we can. Okay?" One of them interrupted him. He nodded his head, "Right; sorry to be patronizing. Throw her in the brig then."

"All this for just one unarmed woman? I mean that's a lot of precautions. I must ask, why bring me onboard it all?" She spoke up with that smile still on her face. Calvin turned around and looked over at her, "So you got good hearing. Can even talk, too! Care to give me a name?"

"You can call me Sophia," she told him plainly. "Why did you attack us?"

She laughed, "Because I had to make my disappearance look convincing to my former government."

"What?" They all asked at once in confusion.

Calvin's eyes narrowed, "Know a person by the name of Holly?"

"She's the one I'm here to see. You're welcome for saving your asses." She told him. He gasped, "Saving? We just lost a shit load of our friends and almost became zombie food! Not to mention fucking up our home system, too! How was that helpful?"

She laughed, "You're not dead. It worked. No one that counts will suspect a thing."

Calvin lifted his hands to his face and dragged them down grumbling, "Fucking kidding me?"

"Only if you want me to. Now I want better accommodations than a brig. How about the CO's quarters? He isn't going to need it seeing how he's dead. Be kind, and have it cleaned. While you're at it, bring me something edible. Heard you have something called Ice Cream that's good. I want to try some," she told them. They all looked at her in confusion. She sighed, "Do I need to call your master?"

"Were not fucking slaves!" Calvin shouted at her as she laughed, "I do understand that you've all had a long few days, but don't push my patience," She told them bluntly. Valery did her best not to cry as she said, "You two clean up the cabin."

They looked at her as Calvin sighed, "Just do it

please."

The two of them walked off mumbling to themselves. Calvin grumbled, "You..., what flavor do you want?"

"Send a sample of each, and then I'll request my favorite. Besides the dessert delivery and Holly, have no one else bother me," she told them as she walked into the ship. Valery pulled off her helmet and face mask. "All this shit was just a damned test?"

"That's the only bullshit that's bothering you?" he asked her as he relaxed his armored suit opening it up. Rotten shouted, "People are fucking dead because of her and that other fucking witch! We're really going to play along with all of this?"

"Know of a way to cut our strings?" Lane asked him. He started to cry, "Fuck!"

"Ice cream sounds good right about now," Calvin said as he walked back toward the passageway. "Everyone else, take a load off. We'll clean up later."

The others stood there in silence as Calvin kept walking toward the mess decks. The other followed him in. They went past the blood covered decks and passageways without paying much attention to the massive amounts of death around them. The mess decks were thankfully clean. Each of them grabbed a tub of ice cream and took a seat. It was cold but melted to the consistency of a shake. Calvin lifted his tub up, "To the fallen!"

The others tapped their cardboard containers together, "Remember them always."

They started to take a long swig of the dessert. They took turns taking sips as they just stared off into the plain white bulkheads. Everything was quiet for once. Calvin nodded to himself, "We did it. We survived."

The others nodded as they kept drinking the ice cream. Calvin laughed to himself, "Deus Ex Machina…"

EPILOGUE

THE six other surviving destroyers flew next to the Jason as they received repairs and supplies from a Claw battle group. It was awkward to say the least seeing former enemies now helping them. Each vessel was busy repairing the damage sustained in the last fight. Calvin was waiting around in the classroom along with Rotten, Lane, and Valery. They all had expressions of being 'burned out' on their faces. They couldn't hide their dissatisfaction at what had just occurred. Valery grumbled, "Hurry up and wait again."

"Witches always have their way," Lane told her as they all looked quietly into the empty classroom. Rotten sighed, "Maybe we should have gotten to know some of our comrades before they were taken away from us. We had some time after all."

"Pardon me if I'm tired of getting attached just to get shattered repeatedly," Valery told him as Calvin wondered, "Better to have something than not at all?"

"Isn't that the age-old question?" Holly asked as the door closed behind her. All four of them stood up at attention, "Ma'am."

"Relax the formalities right now. I just want to talk. Congratulations on a job well done. Once again, a miracle!" She told them while grabbing a drink and offering it to Calvin. "No thank you."

"If I wanted to spike your beverage, I'd tell you it about it then force you to drink it. Lighten up. This is the start of something big. Might not be able to get drunk, but we can still enjoy taste," she told him as she poured herself a glass. "Our guest Sophia sends her regards. Thank you all for being so accommodating."

Lane's eyes opened wide, as she wanted to scream at Holly. Calvin spoke up, "All she had to do was mention her familiarity with you."

"She is the one that saved us! Don't you forget. No need to be a wet blanket. This is only the beginning. Keep in mind what is ahead. We have to deliver on our part," she told them while taking a swig of the champagne. "Soon we'll be back in the Sol system."

"After your friend trashed it?" Rotten pointed out bitterly. Holly scoffed, "Downers! We owe the Spartans nothing. We're now part of a much larger and better organization, one that stretches multiple realities. It's called the Consortium. We'll even get operatives that make you all look like cream puffs! Not that any of you wimps need help in that area. They go by legions. The ones that will be helping are called Mongols, named after the bad asses and most terrifying civilization on Earth, at least in the timelines we're associated with."

"How is this organization going to be any different than the Spartans?" Valery asked humoring her. She smiled, "They've been indoctrinating new timelines for a while now. Clean slate like this one is super easy for them. None of you need to worry about the details."

"Those details seem to bite us in the ass a lot," Rotten mumbled to himself knowing what Holly meant. Calvin sighed, "How is this going to make things better, ma'am?"

"We'll be a fucking force to reckon with! We'll no longer be under the boot heel of anyone else in this universe! Am I getting through to you all?"

"I hear you, ma'am. You want more power," Calvin told her plainly. She nodded, "It is a perk of the plan. All of you will benefit, too. Everyone here is getting a promotion! Chiefs! All of you!"

"Oh joy… ma'am," Valery told her, trying to pretend to be enthusiastic but failing miserably. Holly threw her empty glass to the bulkhead shattering it, "Are you all going soft on me?"

"Ma'am, you can make us do whatever you want. How should we be thrilled knowing that down the line you'll pull our strings again for who knows what?" Calvin asked her, losing his temper. Holly walked up to him, "You have free will... to an extent. You may disobey, but you know very well what fucked up shit I can make you do. I wasn't even using my imagination that last time. Be thankful I didn't make you pull the Aristocrats. Keep performing well, and you'll all reap the benefits. Show signs of dissent and... I'll leave that to your imagination. Those ideas can be very messed up."

"You're going to lead through fear and intimidation?" Valery asked her spitefully. Holly nodded, "We got thrown to the wolves and now we lead the pack. We're never going to get fucked with again when this is over. The old humanity failed and must be swept aside for the new to rise. They may join us if they want to, but I'm not going to have any more hindrances to progress. For too long we held back, and it's bitten our asses. I'll throw you all a bone and leave you out of the conversions, because you all are soft inside. Call me a witch and a monster all you want. The Claws were going to use us as scapegoats, the Vegans were holding us back, and the old humanity abandoned us. I feel no sadness seeing them get thrown under the bus for doing the same to us. Am I clear?"

"Yes ma'am," they replied. She took a swig right of the champagne bottle, "Calvin and Lane, I want you both in my quarters in three hours. Enjoy your time off everyone! Get used to the new doctrine."

"No disrespect, ma'am, but what of Irene and Sophia? They're just as conniving and amoral as you are. How can we trust them?" Valery asked her as Holly laughed, "You can't. Always expect a knife in the back."

She gave them a wink, and walked out of the classroom. "You'll be briefed when we reach the Sol system. Now get our numbers back up. You all know what I'm talking about."

The doors closed, and Lane asked, "When did we become the bad guys?"

"When were we ever good?" Rotten asked as he sat down. Valery kicked over one of the seats, "This is bullshit!"

"There is always a way out." Calvin told them. They all looked over at him. "We survived getting yanked around timelines, suicide missions and zombies. We'll find a way to cut our strings, for true freedom this time."

"I can hear you. Nice try!" Holly's voice came over the intercom. Calvin nodded in defeat and dread, "Well, that was worth a shot. Who wants to get boozed up? Drink them while we got them, right?" Calvin asked as he grabbed a bottle.

Valery threw a bottle against the wall. Rotten followed by breaking a holo-projector. All of them smiled as they broke more and more items in the classroom. The metal seats were ripped apart, the wooden tables shattered on the bulkheads, and the projectors sent sparks flying around. They laughed at the destruction they caused, knowing it was the only act of freedom they had left.

www.ingramcontent.com/pod-product-compliance
Lightning Source LLC
Chambersburg PA
CBHW060323260626
47160CB00007B/2668